MURDER

AT THE RACES

A deadly heist baffles detectives
in this Irish mystery

DAVID PEARSON

THE
BOOK
FOLKS

Paperback edition published by

The Book Folks

London, 2019

© David Pearson

ISBN 978-1-6901-3461-9

www.thebookfolks.com

To Denis and Anne,
for their tireless support and encouragement.

Prologue

Superintendent Mick Hays was presiding over the last logistics meeting in advance of the Galway Races, which would start on the following Monday at Ballybrit Racecourse. The race meeting, which lasts for a full seven days, is by far the most prestigious in the Irish racing calendar, and draws crowds of up to 250,000 as well as breeders, trainers and jockeys from Ireland, the United Kingdom, the Continent, and occasionally even the United States of America.

Chief Superintendent Finbarr Plunkett had asked Hays to look after the arrangements for the event as he would be tied up with other important matters, although, as Detective Superintendent, Hays' remit didn't actually run to large crowd control events. That was normally the responsibility of the man in charge of the uniformed division in the western region of the force, Superintendent Anselm Brennan. But Brennan had been unwell of late, and was on sick leave a good deal of the time, so it had been decided that Hays was better positioned to do the honours.

For the Gardaí, the race festival was a mixed blessing. The local force enjoyed the energy and entertainment that it brought to the city streets, but it meant a lot more work for them. Traffic management was usually chaotic, the roads around the city never having been designed to accommodate such an influx. The quantities of drink consumed in every single bar, restaurant and hotel during the week were simply unbelievable, and this brought its own overhead in terms of managing a certain amount of drunkenness and silliness amongst the party goers.

To assist in this not insignificant task, 120 additional uniformed officers had been drafted in from the surrounding areas. They had come from as far away as Donegal, Athlone and Limerick, and of course these men had to be housed, fed, and watered, as well as being rostered and overseen to ensure the most effective use of the additional manpower.

* * *

Senior Inspector Maureen Lyons was just finishing her report on the series of house break-ins that they had been experiencing recently when Hays came into her office. Hays and Lyons were life partners, living together in Hays' house out in Salthill. They had become a couple some years ago during a visit to Poland when they were tracking the murderer of a Polish student, and although it was unconventional for two senior detectives to have such a relationship, it had worked well for them, and was tolerated by senior management.

"Hi, Mick. Meeting over?"

"God give me strength! If it's not that genius from the Chamber giving me grief, it's the smart arse from the

Hotel Federation. No one wants to take any responsibility for themselves anymore. It's all down to us to sort out. Anyway, glad you finally nailed those two rascals for the house jobs. At least one of us is having some success."

"Will they do time?"

"Ah, you know what Judge Meehan is like with these types. He'll probably give them four weeks community service and a slap on the wrist. But they won't be back here in a hurry. Eamon Flynn put manners on the pair of them!"

Inspector Eamon Flynn was Lyons' right-hand man. He wasn't usually overly aggressive, but the two lads had rightly annoyed him giving the Gardaí the run around over several months, so when he got the chance for a little one-on-one with them, he put the fear of God into them.

"I don't think I want to know, Maureen. Anyway, what about a bite to eat somewhere. I'm famished."

"You say all the right things, Superintendent. I'll just log out here and then let's go."

Chapter One

The races had got off to a really good start. The weather had been kind, and the crowds had thronged to the racecourse in droves. The bars and restaurants were all doing well, and even the bookies had little to complain about, with the amounts being wagered well up on the previous year.

John Durnan was one of the regular turf accountants to attend the festival. He was a man in his early fifties who had taken the business over from his father when he had retired ten years previously. He travelled the country setting up his stall at several of the regular meetings held across the land, but he had a particular soft spot for Galway, coming from not far outside the county himself.

Durnan, like the rest of the bookies, made their book to return a premium of around ten percent of the bets laid, regardless of which horse won any race. This was done by calculating the actual odds for each runner, and then knocking their offer back a notch to ensure a margin. But Durnan had gone one better. Of late, he had taken on a horse in each race, and had increased his takings as a result. He studied the field carefully, and elected a horse that he calculated had little chance of success. This selection would be based on the horse's form and information received, sometimes from the stable hands at the trainer's yard, or occasionally from one of the jockeys. Durnan would then offer much better odds on that horse than the other bookies in the betting ring, and as a result, draw a large number of bets onto the animal. Usually, in fact almost without fail, Durnan's chosen nag would come in well down the field, and as a result, he could increase his margin very substantially.

This particular year, betting at the Galway Races had been significantly higher than in previous years. It was not unusual for bets running to several thousand euros to be placed on a single horse by a single punter, and while the bookies' take was a well-guarded secret, many of them would be heading home with tens of thousands in their brown leather bags. Durnan, with his added advantage, had reaped even more than that in the first two days, and it looked as if his good fortune would continue for the rest of the week.

As the crowds began to disperse at the end of the second day, Durnan was getting ready to leave for home. He packed away the electronics from his pitch and gave the kit to Ronan, his clerk, to take away. He took the brown leather hold-all, which was like an old-fashioned doctor's bag, stuffed with cash, and set off towards his car. But before he reached the car park, as was his habit, he made a diversion to the rear of the grandstand where toilets were located, to relieve himself. He stood alone at the urinals, with the bag of money wedged between his ankles. The sound of the running water and his own bodily functions disguised the almost silent approach of the man coming up behind him. A second later, he had been whacked hard across the back of his head, and slumped awkwardly to the wet floor, hitting his skull hard on the urinal as he went down. He was out cold.

A few minutes later, one of the catering workers entered the gents and found Durnan lying in a pool of his own blood, clearly in a bad way. He dialled 999 on his mobile phone and asked for an ambulance.

Fortunately, the ambulance crews who had been on stand-by in case a jockey took a tumble, hadn't left the racecourse when the call came through, so it only took them two minutes to get to Durnan's side.

The senior paramedic bent down beside the prone form of the bookmaker and started to search for vital signs.

"He's still breathing, Jane, but his pulse is weak. Get some oxygen in here and get the stretcher. We need to get him out of here as soon as we can," the man said.

Jane, herself a highly trained paramedic, went back outside and summoned help from another member of the team. They brought a fibreglass stretcher into the toilets, manoeuvring carefully in the tight space.

"Right, let's get him out into the ambulance. I don't like the way he's looking, and his breathing is very weak. Prepare a saline drip, and keep the oxygen going," the senior man instructed.

A few minutes later, Durnan was stretched out, connected up to the onboard equipment in the back of the ambulance, which was slicing through the busy evening traffic on its way to the regional hospital out by the university. Electrodes had been attached to his chest, and another of the paramedic team was working on him to stop the blood loss from the back of his head. A needle had been injected into the back of his hand for a canula, and he'd been given Adrenalin too – in an effort to keep his heart pumping.

* * *

Detective Inspector Maureen Lyons was in her office packing up her things and getting ready to go home. She was feeling quite pleased that they had got to the end of day two of the racing festival without any major incident. The uniformed Gardaí had been busy managing the crowds that flowed into the town, but the detectives had not been troubled, up to now at least. The additional CCTV and other measures that the racecourse manager had put in place to deter pickpockets seemed to be working well, much to her relief. Then her phone rang.

"Lyons," she said.

"Ah, Inspector, glad to have caught you. This is Sergeant Wallace out at the racecourse. The ambulance crew have just taken a man away to the hospital. It seems he may have been attacked in the gents' toilet at the back of the stands. I have two men guarding the scene for now, but I thought you should know."

"Thanks, Sergeant. Do we know who the man is?" Lyons asked.

"We're not one hundred percent certain, but the person who found him says he thinks it might be one of the bookies. He's not sure, but he thinks he recognises him from coming into the restaurant."

"Right. Well, get that chap's details and ask him to hold on till we get there, will you? I'll be out directly. The back of the stands, you said?"

"Yes, there are both men's and women's toilets here. You can drive right round to them."

"OK. Well, be sure to secure the area till we get there, and see if you can find any sign of a weapon, if one was used. See you soon."

There was some serious traffic congestion on the road out to the racecourse at Ballybrit. Even with the blue lights and the siren working on Lyons' Volvo, progress was slow. Most of the vehicles were coming against them, but several drivers had taken to the wrong side of the narrow road to try and escape the jams, and then had nowhere to go when Lyons came along towards them.

Lyons had brought Detective Sergeant Sally Fahy with her in the car. Fahy had joined the Galway Detective Unit a few years ago, having originally been a civilian worker with the Gardaí. She had enjoyed the work so much that it had taken little persuasion to get her to apply to become a full member of the force, and when she had been trained, Superintendent Hays had pulled a few strings to get her allocated to his team in Galway.

"Sally, will you call Eamon Flynn and get him to go out to the hospital? Suggest he takes someone with him too. Ask him to see if he can talk to the victim – find out anything he can about the attack. He'll know what to do," Lyons said to her passenger.

Eamon Flynn had been with the Galway team for some time, and had been made up to Inspector when Hays had expanded the squad a couple of years earlier. He was renowned for his tenaciousness, never giving up on a hunch or an evidence trail until he got a result.

Fahy made the call, and told Lyons that Flynn was on his way.

"Thanks. Now, let's get forensics out here too. There may be some trace evidence at the scene of the attack that could be useful. Give Sinéad a call if she hasn't gone home already."

Fahy dialled Sinéad Loughran's mobile number.

"Hi, Sinéad, it's Sally Fahy here. I'm on the way out to the racecourse with Inspector Lyons. There's been some sort of attack in the gents' toilet at the back of the stands. Can you come out and see if you can gather any evidence for us?"

"OK, Sally. I'll bring Eddie with me. What's the traffic like?"

"Pretty bad to be honest, but it's thinning out now. See you in a few minutes."

Lyons reached the racecourse and drove around as directed to the rear of the main stand, where she could see two uniformed Gardaí in their high-vis jackets. They had put blue and white crime scene tape across the entrance to the toilets.

She got out of the car and approached the two men.

"I'm Senior Inspector Lyons and this is Sergeant Fahy. How long have you been here?"

"Just a few minutes, Inspector" the taller of the two answered.

"And has there been anyone in or out since you got here?" Lyons said.

"No, Inspector. We sent anyone who approached off to the next block."

"Right, well done. Now, can you extend this cordon for me, please. Make it twenty metres all around. There may be some evidence to be found just about where you are standing."

As the two men were tying a new layer of tape around anything that would support it, Sinéad Loughran pulled up in her shiny 4x4 jeep and got out.

"Hi, Maureen. What have we got?" Loughran said.

Lyons filled Loughran in on what they knew so far, which was very little. Loughran and her assistant Eddie donned white scene-of-crime suits, and started the painstaking task of scratching around on the ground looking for any evidence of the attacker.

Lyons noticed a nervous young man lounging up against the wall of the stand a few metres away, and she asked Fahy to go and have a word with him.

Just as Fahy walked away, Lyons' phone rang. She could see from the screen that it was Eamon Flynn calling.

"Yes, Eamon. I'm out at the racecourse now. How are things there?" Lyons said.

"Not good, boss. Yer man was pronounced dead a few minutes ago. They think he probably died in the ambulance, but they were still working on him when they got him in here. But he's gone now," Flynn said.

"Shit! So, we have a murder on our hands. Terrific. OK. Well, you know what to do. Gather up all his personal stuff, and you'd better call Dr Dodd and let him know. Have we got an ID for the victim yet?" Lyons said.

"Yes. He's John Durnan. I have an address for him too. It was in his wallet. Do you want me to do the honours?" Flynn said.

"Yes, good idea. I'd better get on to Superintendent Hays and let him know what's happened. He may want to close the racecourse," Lyons said.

Chapter Two

Lyons moved away, out of earshot of the team who were now busy with the crime scene. She called Hays on her mobile.

When Hays answered, she told him of the events that had taken place.

"I'm wondering if we need to close the place. What do you think?" Lyons asked.

"God, Maureen, that would be very severe. Plunkett would go mad. Why do you want to close it?" Hays said.

"Well, a man has been murdered. It looks as if he was probably robbed as well, though we haven't any proof of that for now. But it may well have been the motive. We have no idea who the killer is, and he or she is obviously still on the loose, so people may be at risk."

"Hmm. I see what you mean. Look, let me have a word with Finbarr. I'll call you back. Don't say anything about closing it down just yet," Hays said.

"OK. And, Mick, could you text me the contact details for the course manager. I'd better get him out and put him in the picture."

"Sure, no problem," Hays said.

Sally Fahy came back over to where Lyons was standing when she could see that Lyons was off the phone.

"I had a word with that guy. He works in the bar and restaurant. He says he knew the victim to see and exchange a few words with. Said he was a nice guy, always tipped well. Oh, and he told me that he always had an old brown bag, like a doctor's bag, with him whenever he saw him," Fahy said.

"OK. Can you go walkabout and see if any of the other bookies are still around? Don't say Durnan is dead, just say he's gone to hospital for now. See if they saw anything suspicious, or anyone hanging around that didn't seem to fit. Give me a call if you get anything. Thanks," Lyons said.

Lyons walked back over to where Sinéad Loughran was bent down working at the entrance to the gents' toilet.

"Give me some good news, Sinéad," Lyons said.

"No chance. It's hopeless. Just lots of noise – blurred footprints all over. Nothing inside either, I'm afraid. There's plenty of his blood on the floor, but that's about it. Sorry."

Lyons' phone pinged and she read a message from Superintendent Hays. She phoned him back immediately.

"Hi. What's up?" she said.

"Hi. I've spoken to Plunkett. He's livid. Says there's no way we can close the place. It would be a disaster for the town, and we'd never live it down. He offered more men if you need them, but made it pretty clear that he wanted as little disruption to the race meeting as possible, and tight control on the media. What do you reckon?" Hays said.

"Ah, we'll manage, but it doesn't make things any easier for us. No need for extra men for now – the place is already crawling with uniforms. Look, I'm going to be tied up with this for a good while. I'll see you later – much later," Lyons said.

* * *

Sally Fahy walked around to the front of the stand, and along to the bookies' enclosure. It was a lovely evening, with the sun just starting to go down in the west. A light breeze blew across the racecourse carrying the scent of newly cut grass, and workers were out on the track itself patching up the turf where it had been churned up by the earlier races. Cleaners were walking around picking up rubbish and making the place ready for the next day.

As Fahy approached the area where the bookies set out their stalls, she saw that most of them had gone, leaving their advertising boards and makeshift desks behind. They wanted to preserve their pitches for the next race day. Fahy noticed one man though, Tommy Lynch, she assumed, as that was the name on the hoarding he was dismantling and packing into his car. She walked over to him.

"Good evening. Mr Lynch, is it?" Fahy said.

Lynch looked up from the back of his vehicle, and saw a good-looking blonde woman approaching.

"Tommy, call me Tommy. How can I help?"

Fahy produced her warrant card and introduced herself.

"Can I ask why you're packing everything away, Tommy?"

"Ah, don't be talking! I've had enough of this place. Lost my shirt already. Same every year. I don't know why I bother with it; it has a curse on me."

"So, you won't be back tomorrow?" Fahy said.

"Well, I might come in to watch the races, but I won't be making a book."

"Sorry to hear that, Tommy. Can I ask, do you know John Durnan?"

"Sure, of course I do. Isn't he one of us. Why? What's he done?"

"I'm sorry to tell you, Tommy, but John Durnan appears to have been robbed here earlier, when he was taking a leak in the toilet at the back of the stand. They've taken him away to hospital."

"Merciful hour, that's terrible. So that's what the ambulance was doing here then. I was wondering if one of the jockeys might have been injured. Is John all right?"

"We'll know more later, but can I ask you if you saw anyone hanging around the bookies that looked out of place, or suspicious?"

"Not at all. Sure, they are all just faces to me, love. We concentrate on what we're doing when there's a race on. We don't have time to examine the punters," Lynch said. He chuckled to himself.

"And would you have any idea how much John would have had on him at the end of the day?"

"More than me, anyway, that's for sure. I'd say he would've had a good few quid in that famous Gladstone bag of his. He's a shrewd operator. Nothing untoward, mind. He's just canny."

"So, what are we talking. Five grand? Ten? More?" Fahy said.

15

"Ah, for God's sake, he didn't ask me to count it!" Lynch was thinking how much better Durnan had done than he had at the track that day, and it vexed him. But he went on, "I'd say probably somewhere around twenty, including his float."

"Wow. Quite a haul. What's this about a float?" Fahy asked.

"We all bring a float to the meet. I carry five g's at the start, just in case things go badly in the first few races. John would have had the same, or thereabouts, maybe a bit more."

"And do you keep the float back from last week's takings, Tommy, or how does it work?"

"Ah, no, you couldn't do that. We go along to the bank on the Monday morning and withdraw it. We have to clear the takings away into the bank at the end of the week. You can't be holding big lots of cash at home. The blaggards would take it off you quick as a wink."

"I see. Well, I'd better let you get on. Thanks for your help," Fahy said.

"No bother, and if you see John, tell him I was asking for him, won't you?"

Sally walked back to where Lyons was standing by her car, hoping against hope that Sinéad Loughran would come up with something that could help them find the attacker.

"Hi, boss. Any developments?" Fahy said.

Lyons told Fahy that they had been refused permission to close the racecourse, and they both agreed that it was a bit of a long shot in any case.

"Oh, and Eamon was on from the hospital. Durnan's wife has turned up. I've asked Eamon to talk to her to see if she knows anyone that might have born a grudge against him. But he said she's in bad shape, so he may not be able to get much out of her. And I've been talking to the course manager, Ray Cummins. He's on his way over, in fact I'd say this is him now."

A large 4x4 pulled up beside Lyons' Volvo, and a man in his late forties, dressed in a grey suit and a smart blue shirt and tie with a crest, got out. He was tall and thin, with salt and pepper hair, he was well groomed, and his narrow face was well tanned.

Lyons introduced herself and Sally Fahy to the man, noting that he had a firm handshake.

"Good evening, Inspector. I hear there has been an incident here. What's been going on?" Cummins said.

Lyons explained to the man, and this time didn't spare the fact that the victim had died on the way to hospital.

"Oh my God. That's dreadful. The poor man. I knew him quite well, you know. He's quite a character, or was, I should say. His poor wife. This is terrible. And you think he was robbed?"

Fahy spoke up. "Yes, one of the other bookies said he had his Gladstone bag with him with the day's takings. Could have been quite an amount of ready cash in it, it seems."

"Definitely. John was one of the smartest bookmakers on the course. I wouldn't be surprised to find he had twenty grand in the bag. All ready cash too. Hard to trace."

"Mr Cummins, is there any CCTV around here that might give us a clue as to who the thief was?" Lyons said.

"No. There's none at the back here. We have CCTV out front, but nothing happens back here worth recording. Well, not until now, at least. Sorry."

"You need a visit from our crime prevention people, Mr Cummins. It's usually in the less populated parts of public places that bad things happen, not out front where there are thousands of people milling about," Lyons said.

"Well, your guys said that they wanted cameras out front to spot the pickpockets. We did consult them," Cummins rebutted. "Look, about tomorrow. If some thief has got away with thousands from John's bag, he may be tempted to come back later in the week and repeat the performance. What measures are you putting in place to protect the other bookies and the other vendors on the site?"

"That's not up to me, Mr Cummins. You need to speak to Superintendent Hays about that. He's in control of the uniformed police at the course. John Durnan's murder is what I'm concerned with. I'm sure Superintendent Hays will look after any request for increased protection. Talk to him," Lyons said.

"Very well. If you don't need me for anything else then, I'll get off and make the arrangements," Cummins said.

"Fine. We'll talk later," Lyons said. She hadn't warmed to the man.

When Cummins had sped off in his car, Lyons got Loughran and Fahy together.

"OK folks, there's not much more we can do here tonight. Why don't we wrap it up and reconvene at eight in the morning at the station? There'll be plenty of uniformed Gardaí here overnight anyway to keep an eye on things."

Chapter Three

It was late when Lyons got home that evening. Hays was already there, and had prepared a very colourful chicken salad for her which he had left in the fridge under cling film. She hadn't really noticed, but it was a long time since she had eaten anything, and she was very hungry indeed.

As she sat down to eat, Hays poured her a large glass of crisp white chardonnay to go with the salad.

"Thanks, hun. You're a life-saver. This is smashing," she said.

"You're welcome. I thought you could do with something after the evening you've had. You can tell me all about it when you're finished eating."

Lyons tucked into the food, and when she was finished, sat back in the kitchen chair and sighed.

"That's better. Thanks. Well, what can I say? Mr John Durnan, bookie of this parish, is, I'm afraid, no more. And we have absolutely bugger all to go on, except that his famous Gladstone bag, stuffed full of euros, is missing. That's about it," she said.

"What? No CCTV? No convenient eyewitness who faithfully recorded the number plate of the killer's car as he drove away? No clear fingerprints on the murder weapon? You're slipping up, Lyons!"

"Feck off, Superintendent. I'll send you out there tomorrow and you can find all that for us if you like," she said, smiling.

"No thanks. I'll have the press and Plunkett to deal with. But to be honest, I'd rather be out looking for the bastard than doing all that shite, trying to put a positive spin on things. Cummins has already been on to the boss apparently, and he's not a bit happy. You'd think it was one of us that whacked the poor fella over the head and stole his takings. Anyway, enough for now. Relax. There's nothing more you can do this evening."

"You're right. But seriously, Mick, any ideas?"

"If I were you, I'd use the tried and tested Mick Hays technique of 'follow the money'. It's about all you've got anyway."

"Hmm. You're right. Good thinking. Now, let's go to bed, I'm knackered."

* * *

Lyons was in early the following morning, and quickly gathered Eamon Flynn and Sally Fahy around to discuss the events of the previous evening. Flynn had set up a whiteboard in the open plan with a photograph of John Durnan in happier times, working his pitch at some race meeting or other.

"Eamon, have we heard anything back from forensics?" Lyons said.

"No, boss. I'll give Sinéad a call as soon as the hour is decent and see if they found anything last night."

"OK, thanks. Sally, can you get over to the mortuary and attend the post-mortem? Dodd will be doing it soon after nine, if he follows his usual pattern. Get all the normal stuff, but I doubt if there will be any surprises," Lyons said.

"Right, boss. What are you going to do?" Fahy asked.

"I'm going to take Eamon here and go and see Durnan's wife. She wasn't in a fit state to be helpful last night, but hopefully she will be able to tell us a bit more about how he operated today. And I'm going to ask John to get hold of his bank account details. Superintendent Hays has suggested that we follow the money, and it's not a bad idea."

John O'Connor was a uniformed Garda that worked with the detectives to provide technical services of all kinds for them. He loved exploring a PC or a mobile phone, and seemed to be able to extract masses of information from the flimsiest sources with consummate ease. He had been offered promotion more than once, but had declined, preferring to stay at the lowest rank where he could continue to ply his considerable skills in the technical field.

Just as they were getting ready to leave and go about their assigned tasks, Sinéad Loughran appeared in the doorway.

"Morning, folks. Glad I caught you. Got a minute?" she said in her usual bright and breezy manner.

"Hi, Sinéad. Sure, come in. What have you got?" Lyons said.

Loughran held up a plastic bag which appeared to contain something heavy.

"We were just packing up to go last night when Eddie spotted this lying at the side of the stands on the ground. It was getting dark, so we hadn't seen it earlier."

"What is it?" Flynn asked.

"It's a brick. And it has blood and traces of hair on it. I'd wager it is actually the murder weapon. I haven't had a chance to compare the blood and hair to Durnan's yet. The body won't be over from the hospital for half an hour or so."

"Nice one. Are there many loose bricks lying around out there?" Lyons asked.

"That's the odd thing. No, there aren't. None at all, in fact. The place is remarkably tidy, with nothing like that in evidence."

"That's odd. Do you think the killer might have brought it with him, then?" Sally Fahy said.

"Who knows. That's your job, Sally. But I guess he could have. There's definitely no pile of similar bricks we could see anywhere, and although there is a low wall way off to the side of the stands, it's completely intact. No bricks missing or anything like that."

"Right, well, I know this may sound daft, but we have very little to go on with this one. Can you find out as much as you can about the brick? You know – where it was made; who sells them round and about; is it unusual in any way – that sort of thing?"

"Yes, OK. But I'll do the blood and hair analysis first, if that's OK," Loughran said.

"Yes, of course. Nothing else found, I guess?" Lyons said.

"No, nothing. I'll have a full scene-of-crime report later on, but it will just describe the blood and stuff we found in the toilet, and this, of course."

"OK, thanks Sinéad. When you get the brick cleaned up, send us across some close-up photos of it. Chat later."

Lyons then turned to Sally Fahy.

"Sally, I want you to see if you can track down Durnan's clerk. I think Cummins said his name was Ronan, but I didn't get a surname. He shouldn't be too hard to find in any case. See if he can tell you anything about yesterday that was out of the ordinary, or anything at all, really."

"OK, boss. I'll give you a call if anything crops up."

Chapter Four

John Durnan lived with his wife and a grown-up daughter in a fairly large house not far from Ballinasloe in East Galway. The exact location was called Nutfield Cross, and the property occupied several acres of good, flat grassland where horses could be easily grazed. The property itself was set back from the road. It had been built in the 1990s, and was comprised of a spacious five-bedroomed two-storey house, with five stables to the rear, along with various other outhouses and a large double garage.

Access to the place was through a set of sturdy, electrically operated iron gates at the road, and, on arrival, visitors called the house using the intercom provided, to allow the occupier to activate the gates and admit the caller.

Eamon Flynn had phoned ahead to ensure that Mrs Durnan would be at home, and had made an appointment to see her close to eleven o'clock, explaining that the precise time of their arrival would be dictated by the traffic.

It was just ten past eleven when Lyons swung the Volvo into the entrance, and Flynn got out to do the necessary with the intercom.

The driveway up to the house was formed with compacted grit, and when they got close to the residence itself, they saw that it was enclosed with beech hedging that had been neatly pruned, leaving seven feet or so of protection from the prevailing westerly wind that was ever present in those parts.

As they got out of the car, the front door was opened by a tall, slim, dark-haired girl in her twenties, which the detectives took to be Durnan's daughter.

"Come in, folks. I'm Shauna. Mum is inside."

Shauna led the way to the back of the house, where an expansive kitchen-diner with every possible modern appliance surrounded a solid beech-wood table and six sturdy rail-backed chairs. The windows to the rear of the room looked out onto more fields, which Lyons assumed were also part of the spread.

Mrs Durnan was seated at the table in her dressing gown, looking haggard. Her hair was unkempt, and she had clearly been crying, although beneath her somewhat ravaged appearance, there was a very good-looking woman, with high cheek bones and bright blue eyes.

Lyons introduced Flynn and herself, and discovered that Mrs Durnan's first name was Jessica.

"Shauna, get our visitors some tea or coffee, will you, and I think there is still some of that cake that Eileen brought over last night in the fridge," Jessica Durnan said.

"Thanks, two coffees would be lovely," Lyons said.

Shauna busied herself measuring out fresh coffee grounds into the rather complicated looking machine on the worktop, and retrieving Eileen's cake from the fridge, setting it on the table with two plates and forks for the Gardaí.

"Mrs Durnan, firstly, we are very sorry for your loss. It's a dreadful thing, and rest assured, while I know it's little consolation, we will move heaven and earth to bring the perpetrator to justice," Lyons said.

Jessica Durnan raised a rather sodden tissue to her face and sobbed quietly. Lyons looked at Flynn, who wasn't quite sure how they should proceed, but took the hint.

"Mrs Durnan," he said, "we were hoping we could get a bit of information about how your husband ran his business. He was obviously very successful, but we're trying to put together a picture of how he actually operated. Can you tell us about that?"

"I'm not sure, to be honest, but Shauna here would have more of an idea about the day-to-day stuff. She used to go with him to the race meetings when she was younger and help out," Jessica Durnan said. She turned to look at her daughter who was just finalising the coffee arrangements, the machine having finally stopped gurgling and hissing.

"Yes, I went with Dad a lot. He was all over the country, you know. There are two or three race meetings a week in Ireland, and dad went to them all, except Punchestown. He used to say that the place was cursed – he never made any money there, so he stopped going after a while," Shauna said.

"So, can you describe a typical day for us?" Flynn said.

"Well, dad spent a lot of time studying the form of the horses that would be running on the day. You know, their past performance; the weight they would be carrying;

which jockeys were going to be there; and, of course, anything he could find out about the trainers. Then, when we got to the racetrack, he would set up his pitch in the ring and chalk up the odds he had calculated for the first race. After that, it was all much the same. Punters laid their bets. He gave each one a ticket. The clerk wrote the bets into the big ledger he carried with him. Sometimes he would need to lay off some of the money with other bookies, and then we'd watch the race. Once the loudspeaker had declared 'winner all right', he'd start to pay out the winnings to the lucky ones. That's about it, really."

"And what amounts are typically wagered?" Lyons asked.

"Oh, it varied enormously. Some bets were just five or ten euro, but quite often you'd see bets running into the hundreds, and at the big meetings, even thousands. Dad was never shy about taking on big bets, he knew what he was doing. And he knew most of the runners by sight," Shauna said.

"Runners?" Flynn said.

"Yes. The really big gamblers employ runners to place lots of bets just before the off, so that they get the best possible odds. If they can get a load of money down at, say, five to one before the bookies realise what's happening, they can make a killing if the horse romps home. The starting price would probably be only something like two or three to one, or perhaps evens, but if they're holding a ticket at five to one – well, you can see. Dad used to refuse to take some of them. That really annoyed them."

"Was there anyone in particular that got very browned off?" Lyons said.

"Nah. No one special. It's a game, and everyone knows it. Punters versus bookies. An ongoing battle, but thankfully the bookies usually win. Except this time," Shauna said, and her eyes filled with tears.

Lyons and Flynn busied themselves with the coffee and cake for a few moments while Shauna composed herself. When she was a bit steadier, Lyons went on, "And what about the money?"

"What about it?" Shauna said.

"How did it work?" Lyons said.

"Oh, I see, sorry. On the morning of the meeting, Dad would go to the bank and draw out a float. This was in case he had to pay out more than he took in on the first couple of races. Then, as the day went by, he would accumulate cash in his Gladstone bag, and at the end of the meeting we would pack the notes into a small leather pouch that he had got from the bank, and deposit it in the night safe on the way home. He didn't like to keep much cash lying around. 'Too many buggers keen to take it off you these days,' he used to say."

"How much would the float be, Shauna?" Lyons asked.

"It depended on what meeting he was going to. For the big meets like Galway, it could be five thousand or more. He always insisted that the bank gave him new notes for his float. He said it made it easier at the end of the day when he did his tally. He could see how much of the float was left, and how much he had given out."

"Did he have to pay the racetrack to have his pitch?" Flynn asked.

"Yes, of course, except at some of the really small courses. But usually, yes. He paid the course manager, mostly in cash. That came out of his float too."

"I know this is a sensitive question, Shauna, and you don't have to answer if you'd prefer not to, but how much did he usually bring home after a meeting?" Lyons asked.

Shauna looked at her mother.

"It's OK, love. What does it matter now anyway," Jessica said.

"It varied a lot. Sometimes he would complain that it wasn't worth his while going. He'd barely cover expenses. That was at the small evening meetings mostly. But at the big meetings, he often banked ten or twenty grand after he'd paid Ronan, the course fees and all the punters. Galway was always a good meeting for us, though. He often said it was better than Leopardstown for the bookies."

"Thanks, Shauna. Is there anything else at all you can tell us about how your dad's business worked? Did he have any enemies that you're aware of? Anyone with a grudge?" Flynn said.

"No one special. You'd get the odd punter who had lost the kitchen sink on a horse that would shout a few curses at the bookies, but it was just a few hotheads. Nothing serious."

"OK, thanks. Just one more question, Mrs Durnan. Did John have any life assurance?" Flynn asked.

Jessica Durnan dissolved into a fit of crying.

"I can answer that," Shauna said. She moved over to her mother and put an arm around her shoulder.

"Yes, he did. He was always careful to look after us, and he sometimes joked that he was worth more dead than alive. He had a life policy, and if I remember rightly, it was for €250,000. The policy will be in his filing cabinet in the office here. Do you want to see it?"

"No, no, that's fine. Look, we're sorry to have troubled you. I know this is very difficult. Thanks for being so helpful. We'll be in touch when we get the all clear to arrange the funeral," Lyons said.

The two detectives got up from the table, and Shauna led them to the front door.

At the door, Lyons turned to Shauna.

"Just one final question, Shauna. Which bank did your father use?"

"The National in Ballinasloe. Ted Maguire is the manager. He knows us pretty well."

"Thanks, Shauna, you've been very helpful. Is there someone you can get to come over to be with you both – maybe a relative, or your boyfriend?" Lyons said.

"No, we'll be fine, and I don't have a boyfriend, thanks all the same."

"Well, look after her," Lyons said.

"I will."

As Flynn and Lyons approached the wrought iron gates at the bottom of the long drive, they began to swing inwards slowly.

"Where to now?" Flynn said.

"Give you one guess," Lyons replied.

"Should I call ahead and see if he's free?"

"No, I don't think so. Let's surprise him!"

Chapter Five

The National Bank was in the middle of the main street in Ballinasloe. Lyons parked her Volvo at an angle to the kerb and put the small sign showing that she was on Garda business in the windscreen to prevent parking wardens from ticketing it.

Inside the bank, Lyons asked to speak to Mr Maguire. The two of them were requested to take a seat, and, a minute later, a short man in his early fifties in a rather crumpled grey suit with spectacles and short, curly grey hair approached.

"Inspector Lyons, Inspector Flynn, how can I help?" the man said.

"Is there somewhere we could have a word, Mr Maguire?" Flynn said.

"Yes, of course. My office is just down here."

Maguire led the way to the back of the building, where a small but functional office was located. The office was tidy, and the furniture, although not new, was in excellent condition. A faint smell of furniture polish filled the air.

"Can I get you a tea or a coffee?" Maguire asked when they were all seated.

"No thanks. We're fine," the two Gardaí said in unison.

"So, what's this all about, then?"

"We are here in connection with a Mr John Durnan. We understand he's a client here," Flynn said.

"Yes, that's right. John has been with us for a good few years now. Nice man."

"So, you haven't heard then, I take it?" Lyons said.

"Heard what?" Maguire said, a touch of alarm showing in his expression.

"I'm afraid Mr Durnan was the victim of a very serious assault last night out at the Galway Races. I'm sorry to say he didn't make it," Lyons said.

"Oh, dear. Oh my God. That's dreadful. Good Lord, his poor wife, and his daughter. What happened?" the man said.

"We're not in a position to go into detail at the moment, Mr Maguire. We just need to find out a little about his relationship with the bank, and his business operations," Lyons said.

"Well, of course, I'll tell you what I can. But Mr Durnan's account was operated perfectly normally. He had no loans and he wasn't overdrawn, in fact his balance was pretty healthy last time I looked. God, this is terrible. I can't believe the man is dead."

"We understand that Mr Durnan was in the habit of withdrawing a float on the days he was working at the races, and that he usually insisted on new notes," Flynn said.

"Yes, that's right. We always tried to facilitate him whenever possible."

"I wonder if you could check for us how much he drew out on Monday morning, and, if possible, what denominations he took?" Flynn said.

"Hmm, OK. I'll just ask Emma. She would have looked after him on Monday," Maguire said. He made a call on his desk phone and spoke to the cashier. A moment later, a girl appeared in the doorway.

"Emma, I wonder if you could check something for me? Mr Durnan withdrew cash on Monday morning. Could you find out how much, and in what denominations please?" Maguire said.

"Yes, of course, Mr Maguire. It will just take me a few minutes," the girl said, and was gone again.

"You know, I was thinking, Mr Maguire, if Mr Durnan always got new notes, is there a possibility that you might be able to ascertain the serial numbers?" Flynn said.

"Hmm. Maybe. I'm not sure, to be honest. But we can ask Emma when she comes back. She looks after most of our cash handling. It's diminishing rapidly, you know. I remember when I was appointed manager here initially, it was all cash, and lots of it. Especially around the time of the horse fairs, the place would be swimming in it. But not these days. It's all plastic and tap-and-go now," the man said, a little wistfully.

Emma re-appeared a minute later with a page torn from a spiral notebook in her hand.

"Yes, Emma, what have you got?" Maguire asked.

The girl stayed where she was in the doorway and offered the piece of paper to Lyons who was nearest to her.

"Mr Durnan took out €5,000 in new fifties on Monday. I dealt with him myself. The cash was still in the plastic wrapper when I gave it to him, and he put it into his old leather bag."

"There you are," Maguire said cheerfully, "I told you Emma would have the details. Now, Emma, the officers were wondering if by any chance you would have a record of the serial numbers of the notes Mr Durnan withdrew?"

"Perhaps. It will take me a while to sort out though, and the bank is getting busy now." She looked over her left shoulder to confirm to herself that there were indeed queues forming at the two teller hatches.

Lyons took a business card out from her jacket pocket and handed it to her.

"That's fine, Emma. Whatever you can find out could be useful. You can send the details to me later. My email address is on the card. Thanks," Lyons said.

"Well, I think that will be all for now, Mr Maguire. Thank you for your help. We'll be in touch again if we need anything further," Flynn said.

The two detectives stood up and shook hands with the manager and left.

* * *

When Lyons got back to her office in the early afternoon, there was a Post-it Note stuck to her PC saying that an Inspector Hamill would like her to call him. It was a Dublin phone number.

Curious, she dialled the number and waited.

The phone was answered promptly, and then there were some technical noises before she was put through.

"Frank Hamill," the voice at the other end said.

"Inspector Hamill, this is Senior Inspector Maureen Lyons here from the Galway Detective Unit. I got a message to call you."

"Oh, hello Inspector Lyons, thanks for ringing back, and call me Frank. Yes, I understand that a Mr John Durnan was attacked at the racecourse yesterday and regrettably passed away. Is that right?"

"Yes, that's right. We are investigating the incident now. May I ask what your interest is?"

"I'm attached to the Serious and Organised Crime Unit here in Harcourt Street. Mr Durnan is, or should I say, was, a person of interest to us. Have you any idea who attacked him?"

"I see. No, not yet, it's very early days, but our investigation is active. May I ask what sort of interest you had in Durnan?" Lyons said.

"Look, I'd rather not talk on the phone. Would it be OK if I came down to Galway tomorrow morning? I can send you a file on the secure email in the meantime," Hamill said.

"Yes, of course. I'll have to inform the Superintendent, though, if there's another section of the force getting involved. Is that OK with you?"

"Yes, that's not a problem. He'll get a message from my boss here in any case. Hays, isn't it?"

"Yes, Detective Superintendent Michael Hays. That's him," Lyons said.

"Fine. Well, I'll see you at about ten tomorrow. I'll leave early to avoid the traffic. Thanks."

Lyons hung up the phone and reflected on the conversation that had just taken place. She called Flynn on the internal phone and asked him to join her in her office.

Lyons related the conversation she had had with Hamill.

"What do you make of it?" she said.

"Curious all right. But, boss, I was thinking, Durnan seems to have been terribly well-heeled for a bookie. I mean, I know they do OK, but that house, the land – all seems a bit OTT for a bookmaker, don't you think?" Flynn said.

"Hmm. Maybe. His wife could have money. She sounds as if she came from a good family, or maybe he was just very good at what he did."

"Yeah, and maybe there's something else going on. Let's see what Hamill has to say tomorrow."

Chapter Six

Soon after four, Lyons received a call from Sinéad Loughran.

"Hi, Maureen. You know that brick we took from the racecourse? Well, I did as you asked. I got it cleaned up and we found a maker's name stamped into it. It was manufactured in the North of Ireland."

"I see. Is that unusual? I don't know much about the brick business, I'm afraid," Lyons said.

"Apparently, not at all. The building trade get their bricks from all over. There was a code number on it too, so I have someone talking to the makers now to see if they can tell us when it was made or who it was sold to. But don't get your hopes up – they make over a million bricks a year, it seems."

"Terrific. Anything else from the scene?"

"No, not a thing. It's his blood and hair on the brick, so that was definitely the murder weapon, but that's as much as we have. I'm sorry – not much help."

"Nothing from any of the cameras around the front? No one leaving the place at about the right time or anything?" Lyons said.

"No. The course doesn't make any attempt to control the departing vehicles once the races are over for the day. People just want to get away as quickly as they can, so they open all the exits. Some of your boys direct the traffic at the gates, but I doubt they saw anything out of the ordinary."

"OK. Thanks, Sinéad. Talk soon."

Just as Lyons was finishing the conversation, her PC pinged with a new email. It was from the girl at the National Bank. Emma had been able to identify the serial numbers of the banknotes that Durnan had been given at the start of the week, and the list was attached to the email. They were consecutively numbered, one hundred notes in all.

She printed off the list and called John O'Connor in.

"John, this is a list of the serial numbers for the new fifty euro notes that John Durnan drew from the bank on Monday. Can you circulate it to all the stations in the area, and the banks too? I want to know as soon as one or more of them turn up."

"Yes. Sure, boss."

"Oh, and is Sally outside?"

"Yes. She's at her desk. Shall I ask her to pop in?" O'Connor said.

"Yes, please. Thanks."

A moment later, Sally Fahy appeared at the door.

"Come in, Sally, grab a seat," Lyons said.

"Thanks, boss. What's up?"

"This damn case is what's up. We've made little progress. And now some hot shot from the Serious Crime Squad in Dublin is trying to muscle in. If we don't start getting somewhere soon, we're going to look like bloody country bumpkins."

"It's not that bad, surely? It's only just happened, after all. But I know what you mean about no leads. Any ideas?"

"Maybe. I have to be here tomorrow to see this Inspector Hamill from Dublin. But I was wondering if you and Eamon could schlep over to Ballinasloe again and talk to Shauna Durnan. Download a couple of images of Gladstone bags from the web, and get her to identify the picture that is closest to her dad's bag. We might be able to get it on TV. Whoever took his cash won't be too keen to hang on to the bag, it's too distinctive."

"OK. I can do that, sure. Anything else?"

Lyons told Fahy about the serial numbers from the notes.

"Well, that should bring something, but it will take a few days. Are you feeling restless?"

"Very!"

"I know what you need, Inspector Lyons," Fahy said smiling.

"What?"

"Alcohol. C'mon. Let's go across the road and get a glass or two of chardonnay inside us. That'll make you feel better."

"You know, I think you may just be right. Give me ten minutes," Lyons said.

* * *

Fahy and Lyons were seated at a small table in Doherty's pub close to the Garda station at Mill Street with a large glass of white wine in front of each of them and a small bowl of dry roasted peanuts between them.

"So, how's the love life?" Lyons asked her sergeant.

"Don't, will ye. You've heard of a drought. Well, think of the Sahara Desert. That just about sums it up."

"That good, eh? Maybe Inspector Hamill from Dublin will sweep you off your feet."

"Yeah, and that's why you're sending me to bloody Ballinasloe early doors, so I won't even get to see the fecker," Fahy said jokingly.

"Well, I could detain him for you, if you like. How would you like him? Handcuffed? In a cell?"

"Stop! You're incorrigible, Maureen Lyons." They both laughed out loud.

Mick Hays came in to the pub and made his way over to where the two women were seated.

"I thought I might find you here," he said. He grabbed another stool from a nearby table that was unoccupied, and sat down between them.

"Can I get you a drink, sir?" Fahy said.

"No thanks, Sally. And it's Mick when we're off duty. Liam is pulling me a pint of Guinness. What about you two. Ready for another?"

"We're fine for now, thanks," Lyons said.

"So, what's happening with this Durnan thing? I hear we are having a visit from the Smoke tomorrow," Hays said.

"We were just saying we haven't a clue, but don't quote me on that. Sally is going to go back to the family and see if we can get a good picture of the bag he was carrying. We thought you might be able to get it on TV," Lyons said.

"Good idea."

The barman came across and placed Hays' pint in front of him.

"Thanks, Liam. Get these two another as well, will you?" Hays said. He looked at Lyons for confirmation.

"Well, if you insist. Thanks," Lyons said, and both of the women raised their glasses in a mock toast as Hays took the first sip of his creamy pint.

"Have you any ideas, sir – I mean, Mick?" Fahy said.

"You know me. I'd say follow the money. See if any of the local boys are splashing it around at all, or buying a new car for cash – something flash. Whoever it was will hardly be putting all those readies into a savings account. And this guy from Dublin could have something interesting to say as well. He won't be coming down just for the day out."

"That's a good idea. I'll give Eamon a call and ask him to put the word out amongst the shadier car dealers. Do you think we could get a reward organised for information leading to an arrest or whatever, Mick?" Lyons said.

"Probably. But it's a bit soon. Let's see what we can turn up in the next week or so, and if there's still nothing happening, we could probably put something up."

The little group stayed in the pub for another half-hour and then went their separate ways. Fahy was fascinated to see the interaction between the two more senior officers who were also a couple. She couldn't help but be a little bit envious.

* * *

On the way back to their home in Salthill, Hays asked Lyons how Fahy was doing.

"She's great. It's good to have another girl on the team that I can rely on. Eamon is terrific too, but he's a guy, and it does make a difference sometimes. Why do you ask?"

"Well, she's been a sergeant for quite a while now. Do you think she's due a promotion?"

"No, I think it's a bit too soon, to be honest. There's nothing wrong with her work, but she needs more time to develop a good detecting instinct. She'd do anything for you, and never complains – well, not much anyway – but her 'nose' isn't working fully yet."

"Do you think she'll make it?"

"Almost certainly. Maybe I'll try and stretch her a bit and see how she responds if you like. Why are you so keen to move her up?"

"Ah, you know how it is. The chiefs are asking us to get more female officers into the higher ranks. Gender balance and all that. You know we have to be ever so politically correct these days," Hays said.

"Why? Am I not enough for them?"

"I think you scare the hell out of them, Maureen. You should hear some of the comments I've heard when your performance comes up for discussion. They know you get fantastic results, it's just your methods that sometimes cause raised eyebrows."

"Well, I'm never going to apologise for that. I haven't let a killer slip through my hands yet, thanks to your support."

Hays reached across and took her hand in his.

"That's my girl."

Chapter Seven

Lyons was at her desk the following morning, answering emails and updating the duty rosters for her team. They had all put in a good bit of overtime recently, and she wondered if she would get a sideswipe from above about the expenditure. At ten o'clock on the button, her desk phone rang.

"Good morning, Inspector. It's the front desk here. I have an Inspector Frank Hamill here asking for you," O'Toole, the desk sergeant, said.

"Oh, thanks, Dermot, I'll be down right away."

Frank Hamill was seated in the waiting area, thumbing through a copy of *The Connaught Tribune,* when Lyons arrived down to collect him. Hamill was tall – very tall – probably about six foot three inches by Lyons' reckoning, and he was very slim. He had brown hair going grey at the temples, and he was clean-shaven with a long, narrow, and quite weather-beaten face. He was wearing stone-coloured chinos, a navy polo shirt and a tan leather jacket. Lyons observed that he had good black leather shoes that were highly polished.

"Good morning, Inspector," Lyons said extending her hand.

"Inspector Lyons, I presume. Do call me Frank, and it's Maureen, isn't it?"

"Yes, Maureen is fine. Let's go to my office. Did you have a good drive down?"

"Yes, thanks, dry all the way, and the sun was behind me. There was very little traffic too. I got here sooner than I thought."

When they reached her office, Hamill sat opposite Lyons, who tucked in behind her desk. As she sat down, her PC pinged, and she saw that there was a new email from Hays in her inbox.

"Excuse me a moment while I deal with this, Frank," she said.

Hays' email was all about the man sitting opposite her. It read, 'Careful with Hamill. He has a rep for muscling in and taking the credit without doing too much of the donkey work. Watch your back.'

"Anything important?" Hamill asked.

"No, no, it's fine. Just routine," Lyons said, showing no expression on her face.

"So, what can you tell us about John Durnan, Frank?" she said.

"He's come up a few times in our investigation into a particularly nasty gang that's involved with the drug trade. We think he may have been doing a bit of money laundering for them."

"I see. How would that work?"

"This is largely speculation on our part, but we have received some information to back it up. It involves horse racing, as you have probably guessed. Durnan takes a bet on the course of, say, a thousand euro, but he doesn't write it up in his book. The race finishes, and let's say the winner comes in at eight to one. Durnan then writes the bet into his book, and the payout of eight thousand euro to the lucky punter, but he doesn't pay out anything. The gang can then take the eight grand from their stack of drug money and claim they won it at the races – it's clean. The gang keep the betting slip, and by now the bet is written up in Durnan's book, so it all looks legit."

"And what happens to the proceeds of the bet?" Lyons asked.

"Durnan trousers it, because otherwise his accounts wouldn't balance – and the original stake – so, he now has nine grand cash off the books that he can spend as he chooses. If anyone looks at his records, they balance perfectly, and it has only cost the drug dealers a grand to clean eight. Everyone's a winner!" Hamill said.

"Nice. So how often do you think they operate the scam?" Lyons said.

"It's hard to tell, but probably two or three times a month. Durnan wouldn't be their only mark, and of course they'd make sure they lose some bets as well to make it look kosher."

"Hmm, but that leaves Durnan with a pile of ready cash sloshing about. How does he spend it without drawing attention to himself?" Lyons said.

"He's clever. Take his house, for example. We know he spent a lot of money on it three years ago, extending it. We checked with the builder, or rather the builder's accountant. The builder put through eighty-five thousand for the work carried out, but we had the plans looked over by an architect, and he reckons it cost more like a hundred and fifty, so presumably the rest was paid in cash. Same with his cars. His wife drives a big 4x4 that would have cost over sixty thousand new, but it seems he only paid twenty-five for it from a huckster hereabouts."

"I see what you mean. We did think that his lifestyle was a bit ostentatious for a bookie, to be fair," Lyons said.

"Well, now you can see why. We figured he's probably pocketing close to two hundred grand a year. Not bad, and no visible risk," Hamill said.

"Except that someone decided to whack him over the head and snatch his takings, so maybe not as risk-free as it looks. Do you think there's a connection between his criminal friends and the attack?"

"That's what I'm here to find out, Maureen. There could well be. Maybe he got a bit greedy, or perhaps he was blabbing to someone about the scheme and word got back to the gang. Who knows. These boys don't think twice about using violence to make a point, though they may not have intended to actually kill him. Just send a message. But there's something else," Hamill said.

"Go on," Lyons said, sensing a change in tone in Hamill's voice. She knew she wouldn't like what he was about to say.

"If he's been operating this scam as we think he has, then he had a right old stash of cash somewhere that he couldn't lodge to a bank. My guess is it's hidden somewhere around the property," Hamill said.

"I was wondering when you were going to get to that. And I suppose you want us to arrange a search warrant and tear the place apart looking for it?"

Hamill just looked at her and shrugged.

"I don't know, Frank. It's going to look very bad if we go rushing into a victim's house and start ripping up the floorboards and find nothing. Can you imagine what the press would do with that story? And besides, we're completely stretched till the race meeting at Ballybrit is over. Could we not try a bit of proper detective work first – see if we can flush something out?"

"It's your call, Maureen, but our lot won't be too happy if they find out he's been sitting on a bunch of hot money and we didn't find it."

"Let me think about it. How long are you going to be here?" Lyons said.

"Oh, I'll probably stay for a few days. Do a bit of my own sleuthing round and about. But I promise I won't get in your way. You'll hardly know I'm here at all."

"Any definite plans we should know about?" Lyons asked.

"I'm going to go out to the races. Just mingle with the crowd. See if I can pick up anything at all. Sometimes you can get lucky."

"OK. Well, all I ask is that if you do find anything relevant to Durnan's death, you keep me posted sooner rather than later. Here's my card, and you can call me anytime, day or night."

"Thanks. Right then, I'll be off."

As Lyons walked back out to the open plan with Hamill, Sally Fahy and Eamon Flynn arrived back from their excursion to Durnan's house in Ballinasloe.

"Hi, Eamon; Sally. This is Inspector Hamill from Dublin. He's been telling me a bit more about our victim."

The two detectives shook hands with Hamill, and Lyons noticed that he was taking his time to appraise Sally Fahy's neat figure and pretty face. There was an awkward moment when no one spoke, so Lyons decided to fill the gap.

"Inspector Hamill will be here for a few days. He has some enquiries to make, so any assistance we can give him… You know the drill," Lyons said.

Hamill finally peeled his gaze away from the blonde Detective Sergeant, and left.

"So, did you get anything out at Durnan's house?" Lyons said.

"Well, Shauna was able to pick out the Gladstone bag that was most like her old man's. This is it here," Flynn said. He held up one of the photos that Fahy had downloaded from the web earlier.

"Anything else useful?"

"Maybe. While I was having a cup of coffee with Mrs Durnan in the house, Sally went walkabout with Shauna to the stables. Sally, tell the boss what she said."

"Not a lot, really. But she did say that she didn't know how they were going to cope financially now that her father, who was the sole breadwinner, was gone. She said she didn't know how they would be fixed, although her dad's bank balance was healthy enough to tide them over, and there was the insurance. Apparently, Shauna did his accounts."

"Interesting. Let's keep that little nugget to ourselves for now, OK? Particularly, don't tell Hamill, and don't put it in the system for the moment," Lyons said.

Flynn and Fahy exchanged slightly puzzled looks.

"OK, boss. It's in my pocket book in any case," Fahy said.

* * *

When Lyons got back to her office, she put a call through to Mick Hays.

"Mick, it's me. Listen, can you spare me one uniformed Garda for a day or two from all the extra officers you've got?" Lyons said.

"Maybe. What are you up to?"

"Well, you know I'm a sucker for a man in uniform. No, seriously, I want a keen young Garda in a bright yellow jacket outside John Durnan's house for the next few days and nights. Just observing – he doesn't have to do anything more."

"That's three men in uniform, Maureen – if it's 24 hours."

"Two, if you allow them some overtime. Look, I wouldn't ask if it wasn't important. What do you say, Superintendent?"

"Very well. We're swimming in uniformed officers anyway. So, I'll talk to Wallace out at the racecourse and get him to liberate someone. I take it you want it to start as soon as?"

"Give me an hour to brief the Durnans, OK? And thanks."

"You're welcome. What are the instructions for the poor lad or lassie?"

Lyons went on to explain exactly what she wanted the officer to do while ostensibly standing guard at the dead man's home.

Chapter Eight

It was late afternoon before Sergeant Séan Mulholland got around to calling Lyons. Mulholland was the officer in charge of Clifden Garda station, some fifty miles west of Galway city, right out on the coast. Mulholland had his own way of doing things at a gentle pace. As he would sometimes say, when asked why things seemed to take so long to organise, "Sure, when God made time, he made plenty of it!"

"Maureen, it's Séan here in Clifden. Have you got a minute?" he said when she answered the phone.

Although Lyons was now two ranks above Mulholland, they had both been sergeants at the same time some years ago, and they continued to call each other by their first names.

"Hello, Séan. What can I do for you?"

"It's more like what I might be able to do for you, Maureen. You know those fifty euro notes you were asking us all to look out for? Well, one of them has turned up out here. The bank manager called me this morning. It was in the night bag lodgement from the betting shop here in town."

Lyons pondered whether to have a go at him for taking so long to relay the information, but decided that it wouldn't be productive.

"Great, Seán. That's terrific. Have you been down to the bookie's to see if they have any idea who handed it in?" Lyons said, rather hopefully.

"No, I haven't. I've been fairly busy here today. There was a traffic accident down outside Ferris' garage at lunchtime, and we've been tied up with that."

"OK. What time does the bookie's close today?" Lyons said.

"Around six, I think. But Matty lives over the shop in any case, so he'll be around if we need him."

"Seán, can you get on to him straight away and make sure that the CCTV footage from yesterday isn't deleted or overwritten. I'll come out first thing tomorrow and see what we can get from him."

"Oh, right so. I'll give him a call. See you in the morning then."

Lyons knew that Mulholland was in the habit of keeping his own hours at the Garda station. It should stay open from eight in the morning till eight in the evening, but the sergeant often closed up at half past six and went down the street to Cusheen's bar where he would enjoy two or three pints of Guinness and have a read of the paper before heading home to his rather scruffy bungalow just outside the town. Mulholland had never married, and lived on his own, which accounted for his staying on in the Gardaí well beyond retirement age so he could keep active and be amongst the townsfolk.

Eamon Flynn and Sally Fahy were busy organising with the Garda press office to get a photograph of Durnan's Gladstone bag broadcast on the evening news, so Lyons told them about Mulholland's call and left them to it.

When they had finished their efforts, RTÉ having agreed to run the story on the six o'clock news and again at nine, Fahy's mobile phone rang.

"Hi, Sally. This is Frank Hamill here. I was wondering if you were free this evening, maybe we could have dinner together? I'm at a loose end, and I don't know the city very well. Maybe you could suggest somewhere appropriate. My treat of course."

"Oh, hello Inspector. Yes, thank you, that would be very nice. Where are you staying?"

"Call me Frank, Sally. I'm at the Imperial, but I imagine we could do a bit better than that for an evening meal."

"Yes, I agree. Why don't I call for you at, say, seven o'clock, and we can take it from there?"

"Perfect. I'll be waiting in the lobby," Hamill said.

When Sally Fahy had hung up, Flynn said, "Jesus, Sally, you're playing with fire there."

"I'll be fine. But do me a favour, will you?"

"Sure. What?"

"Call me at nine thirty on some pretext. If it's all going pear shaped, I'll use your call as an excuse to get away. But if it's going well, I'll say it can wait till tomorrow. OK?"

"OK. But for God's sake, be careful, girl."

"As in, if I can't be good, be careful?" she said, smiling.

"Get outta here. Enjoy!"

* * *

52

Sally Fahy had just enough time to go home and change her clothes, have a quick shower and freshen up before going to meet Frank Hamill at the hotel. She pondered what to wear for a few minutes, and settled on a light summer dress, a black cardigan, and a pair of open toe sandals. She finished off the ensemble with a small clutch bag just big enough to hold her purse, her pocket book, her warrant card, and her mobile phone. It was a fine, warm evening, and she didn't think she needed a coat or a jacket.

When she got to the Imperial Hotel at ten past seven, Frank Hamill was waiting in the lobby reading the paper.

"Hi, Sally. Wow, you look terrific! Quite a transformation from earlier, if I may say so."

"Well, a girl has to do her best when she's being entertained by a senior officer," Fahy said.

"Oh, forget that, it's just Sally and Frank for this evening, OK?"

"Well, at least it's not Harry!" she said with a twinkle in her eye.

The two walked down along Shop Street where the early evening crowds were bustling along. Halfway down, they turned into a narrow side street where An Béal Bocht, a trendy bistro-like place, occupied the corner opposite the bank. Inside was busy, with almost every table occupied and waiters and waitresses dashing about carrying trays above their heads to avoid bumping into the patrons.

Sally made her way to the bar where the manager was pouring a pinkish coloured mixture into a tall cocktail glass with sugar crystals around the rim.

"Hi, Sally. Don't tell me – you're looking for a table," he said cheerily.

"Hi, Cathal. Any chance?"

"Give me ten minutes and I'll sort you out. Have a drink while you're waiting, and I'll get you a couple of menus," Cathal said. He dashed off carrying the strange concoction he had been mixing aloft while Fahy and Hamill sat up on stools at the bar.

While they sipped their drinks, Hamill asked Fahy about living in Galway. He inquired about her interests outside of work, her family, and circle of friends, and how she had come to join the Gardaí. The conversation flowed easily, and Fahy was beginning to warm to this older man with his relaxed manner and apparent interest in her.

Cathal returned to them ten minutes later as promised, and seated them at a table for two near the back of the restaurant. There was a small candle on the table that made Fahy's eyes sparkle even more than usual.

When they had finished their starters, Sally excused herself to go to the ladies. She was only gone a couple of minutes, and returned to find Frank Hamill bent down almost to floor level reading her pocket book that she had left on view in her bag at the leg of her chair.

"What the fuck do you think you're doing?" she demanded, being careful not to raise her voice.

Hamill straightened up, his face reddening, possibly from embarrassment or maybe from the exertion of the unusual position he had adopted to poke around in her handbag.

"Oh, sorry, I just thought your phone was ringing, and thought I'd better answer it in case it was urgent," he said smoothly.

"Nice try, Frank. But my phone is in my hand. I always keep it with me."

"My mistake. It must have been someone else's then," he said, trying to recover.

Fahy bent down and collected her handbag from the floor. She took a swig of her wine, and retrieved her cardigan from the back of the chair.

"You're not going, are you?" Hamill said.

"Brilliant. I can see why they made you a Detective Inspector!"

"Ah, don't go. It was just a simple misunderstanding. We're all on the same side here, really. Sit down. Finish your meal at least."

Fahy continued to take her leave of the man, but as she side-stepped between the closely packed tables, she swiped Hamill's almost full glass of red wine so that it spilled onto the front of his trousers. The glass continued to the floor where it shattered in several pieces.

"Oops!" she said, and left.

When she got outside, and a good way clear of the restaurant, she phoned Maureen Lyons.

"Hi, Maureen. Sorry to disturb you. Are you at home?"

"Hi, Sally. Yes, sure. It's no bother. We're just in. Mick is just getting the dinner. What's up?"

"Do you think it would be OK if I called around for a few minutes?" Fahy said.

"Yes, sure. I'll set another place. Are you on your way? Are you OK?"

"Yes, I'm fine. I'll tell you when I see you. I'll be there in ten minutes."

"Great. See you then."

* * *

"Hi, Sally. Come in. We're just about to tackle one of Mick's homemade lasagnes. It's his speciality. Red or white?" Lyons said.

"White, thanks. I'm really sorry to barge in, but there's something I think you and the Superintendent should know about."

"Sounds ominous," Lyons said.

Fahy sat down at the table with them. Hays' lasagne was really excellent, and was accompanied by a very colourful salad with olives, peppers, fresh baby tomatoes, lettuce, sun-dried tomatoes, and even some pieces of sweet orange.

As they ate, Fahy told them about what had taken place.

"Cheeky bugger!" Hays said as the tale unfolded. "I'll soon put a stop to his gallop, don't worry."

"God, Mick, I'm not even sure I should have said anything. He'll think I'm a right little snitch if you tackle him over it," Fahy said.

"Don't you worry about that. I'm not having some hot shot wannabee from Dublin coming down here and treating us like gobshites. He can feck off. But don't worry, I'll do it in such a way that there will be no comeback, I promise you," Hays said.

Lyons poured her sergeant another glass of white wine, and they relaxed as they savoured the delicious meal. Fahy was surprised by the man's culinary skills.

"You'd better stay the night, Sally. The spare room is all made up. Don't want you getting pinged for drink-driving. I'll dig out a toothbrush for you, and I have a fresh blouse I can lend you for tomorrow," Lyons said.

"Thanks, Maureen. I've put you to a lot of trouble. I'm sorry."

"Don't be daft, girl. You may, in fact, have saved us a pile of trouble if that's the kind of thing Hamill is up to. I bet he wants to find a way to take the credit when Maureen solves this case," Hays said.

The three of them sat in the lounge finishing the bottle of wine and chatting for a while to let their meal go down. At half past nine on the dot, Fahy's phone rang, and she could see from the screen that it was Eamon Flynn.

"Hi, Eamon. Thanks for calling. I'm actually out at Inspector Lyons' house. I had to leave Hamill a bit earlier," Fahy said.

"Oh, what happened?" Flynn said.

"Ah, I'll tell you tomorrow. Nothing major, but thanks for phoning. I'm grand."

"Right, OK. See you tomorrow then."

Chapter Nine

At half past seven the following morning, Superintendent Mick Hays walked into the dining room at the Imperial Hotel. He hadn't met Hamill, but he instantly recognised him sitting alone at a four-seater table with a full Irish breakfast and a large pot of coffee in front of him.

Hays walked over to Hamill's table.

"Inspector Hamill? I'm Superintendent Hays," he said, pulling out a chair and taking a seat opposite Hamill.

Hamill extended his arm to shake hands with the Superintendent, but Hays did not reciprocate.

"Good morning, Superintendent. I presume you're here to discuss the murder of John Durnan?" Hamill said.

"You presume incorrectly, Inspector. I am here to give you a clear and unambiguous instruction," Hays said.

"Oh. What's that, then?" Hamill said. He buttered another slice of toast, keen to avoid eye contact with Hays.

"When you have finished your breakfast, or sooner if you wish, you will go back to your bedroom and pack your dirty socks and pyjamas into your little case, and then check out of the hotel, settling your bill as you do so. You will then drive back to Dublin, and will have no further contact of any kind with any of my officers in relation to this case, or anything else for that matter. Do you understand?" Hays said.

Hamill went red in the face and stopped eating.

"Is this because of that little tart last night?"

"Is there anything in what I have said that you do not understand, Inspector?"

Hamill said nothing. He removed his linen table napkin from his lap and threw it down on top of his half-eaten meal. He stood up and left the room.

Hays waited in the lobby, and ten minutes later Hamill re-appeared wheeling a small overnight case behind him. He went to the front desk and settled his bill, and then turned to face Hays as he made for the door.

"You haven't heard the last of this, Superintendent. No one treats an inspector from the Serious and Organised Crime Squad like this. I'll be making a formal complaint."

"Two things you should know, Hamill. One – I know exactly what your game is. I know that you intended to grab the credit for solving this case when my team had done all the work on it. And two – your boss, Superintendent Gerry Mulligan, is a good friend of mine. I was his sergeant in Kimmage when he first joined the force, and we've kept in touch ever since. I must give him a call and see how he's doing. I haven't spoken to him for a couple of months. Safe journey now." And with that, Hays turned and left Hamill standing there with his mouth open.

When Hays got back to his car, he made a phone call. He wasn't quite finished with Inspector Hamill yet.

* * *

Hamill was furious. He knew he had been bettered by the Galway detectives, and he didn't like it. For most of his career, he had advanced by letting others do the work and then stepping in at the last minute to claim the credit for either himself, or his small team. As a recipe for success, it had worked well. Officers less senior than himself would never speak out about what was really going on. They were too afraid of losing their jobs, or the rest of the squad closing ranks on them. So, Hamill had got away with it – until today.

His temper didn't abate as he drove along towards Dublin on the M6. The sun was in his eyes as he travelled east, and he didn't notice the speed in his silver BMW increasing steadily, till he was doing over 150 kilometres an hour just past Loughrea. That is, until he saw the white Hyundai with its blue flashing lights in his rear-view mirror.

Hamill pulled over to the hard shoulder and stopped the car. The Garda vehicle pulled in behind him, and a sergeant in shirt sleeves got out and approached. Hamill wound down the window.

"Good morning, sir. In a bit of a hurry, are we?" the burly sergeant said, bending down to get on eye level with the driver.

Hamill held up his warrant card for the sergeant to see.

"I'm in the job, Sergeant. Just got a bit fast on this nice wide, open road," Hamill said.

"Yes, indeed, sir. We clocked you at one hundred and fifty-two. You know that the limit on here is a hundred and twenty, I presume?"

"Yes, of course. I'm sorry. I'll slow down. Thanks for pointing it out."

"And tell me, Inspector, are you actually on your way to a call-out somewhere in these parts? We haven't heard anything on the radio?" the sergeant continued.

"No, Sergeant. I've been doing some work in Galway, and I'm on my way back to Dublin. I'd quite like to get going now."

"Could I just ask you to step out of your car, and take a seat in the back of our car for a few minutes, sir? I need to check a few things," the sergeant said. He reached in through the open window of the BMW and withdrew the key from the ignition.

"What things? You've seen my ID. Is that not enough for you?" Hamill said. He was beginning to feel this whole thing was becoming very tiresome.

"Won't keep you long, sir," the sergeant said, opening the driver's door of Hamill's car.

"For fuck sake," Hamill said as he climbed reluctantly out of the driver's seat.

"Sorry. What was that, sir?"

"Nothing, Sergeant."

When Hamill was seated in the back of the Hyundai, accompanied by a young Garda, the sergeant made a point of telephoning Hamill's unit in Harcourt Street to check the man's identity. He explained the full circumstances of the reason for the call, much to Hamill's discomfort. When the call was over, he turned again to Hamill.

"May I see your driver's license please, Mr Hamill?"

"That's Inspector Hamill to you, Sergeant," Hamill said.

"Oh, sorry, sir. May I see your driver's license please, Inspector Hamill?"

"I don't have it with me. Look, you've seen my warrant card, and you have verified I am who I say I am, so I want to get on with my journey. Now, stop pricking about."

"Well, we know who you are all right, Inspector, but I have no idea if you have a valid driving license, have I now? And Superintendent Hays is very particular about that sort of thing. He always insists we see the license, or issue a fixed penalty notice."

"So, that's your game, is it? Hays – again!"

"So, if you haven't got your license on you, I'll have to issue you with a fixed penalty notice. And because we measured your speed at over 150kph for more than a kilometre, that will be another charge – and that's a mandatory court appearance, here in Loughrea, because of the excessive speed."

"Jesus! This is ridiculous. I'm one of your own. Can you not cut me some slack, Sergeant?"

"Just doing my job, sir. Trying our best to keep the roads safe. You get all sorts of mad stuff going on at this time of year, what with the tourists and all. We could have saved you from a nasty accident."

"Gee – thanks a bunch!" Hamill said.

The sergeant took his time writing up the citations for Hamill and advising him on how to deal with the various tickets he had accumulated. The stop had taken almost half an hour, and had done nothing to soothe Hamill's already foul humour. He'd be glad to get out of County Galway and back home.

When Hamill finally got back into his car and set off at a sedate pace, Sergeant Joyce made a call on his mobile phone.

"Job done, sir. Just as you said, he came tearing along like a bat out of hell, so we nabbed him. He didn't have his license on him either, so he got a second ticket," Joyce said.

"Excellent. Thanks, Liam. Well done," Hays said.

Chapter Ten

It was a glorious summer's day as Lyons and Fahy drove out along the N59 towards Clifden. There wasn't a cloud in the sky, and the searing heat from the sun had melted the tar on the road here and there.

Once they had gone through Oughterard, the sweet smell of the heathland's wildflowers wafted in through the open windows of Lyons' Volvo.

"Thanks a lot for last night, boss. I got a bit of a shock at your man's antics," Fahy said.

"Ah, you're grand, Sally. I think Mick has sorted him out, anyway."

"Yeah. I didn't know he was such a good cook, though. That meal was delicious. Probably better than I was going to have with Hamill!"

"Sure, he's a little treasure, but don't tell him I said that. But, seriously, he's a good man. And they aren't easy to find," Lyons said.

"Tell me about it!"

"And thanks for the loan of your clothes too. They fit me really well," Fahy said. "It wouldn't do to rock up to the Garda station in Clifden in my glad rags."

"You never know, Sally. You might have snagged Séan Mulholland dressed like that!"

"Eh… it's OK, thanks, I think I'll pass on that one."

* * *

It was just after nine when they reached Clifden. The Garda station was open, and when they went inside, they weren't surprised to find that Sergeant Mulholland had the kettle on for tea.

"Ah, good morning, ladies. Just in time for a cuppa," Mulholland said.

As the three of them sat down at the table to have their tea, Lyons opened up the conversation.

"So, what's the story with this banknote, Séan."

"Well, we have the CD from the recorder at the bookie's. But it would be best if we went down and had a chat with them. They're a friendly lot, and Matty will help us if he can."

They all finished their tea, and trooped off down the street to the bookie's shop. The place was deserted, except for Matty, the proprietor, and Mary, who worked behind the counter.

When the introductions had been made, Matty brought everyone into the office at the back of the shop. It was quite crowded with all of them in there, but Lyons and Fahy were offered seats.

Mulholland explained the significance of the fifty euro note that had come from the bookie's night bag.

"Is there any chance that you can remember who brought it in?" Fahy asked.

Mary spoke up. "I do, yeah. It was Dónal Keogh. He's a regular, but he never bets more than a tenner. That's how I remember it. He put the whole fifty on a horse to win at Galway. I asked him if he was sure, but he was insistent, so naturally I took the bet."

"Did his horse win?" Matty asked.

"No, 'course not."

"What do we know about Dónal Keogh?" Lyons asked.

"He's a local. From a good, hard-working family. Dónal works in one of the hotels down near the old station. I think he's in the kitchens. I can't believe he has any connection to what happened, though I know it doesn't look too good," Mulholland said.

"Does he come in every day?" Fahy said.

"Not every day. But he might this week, what with the races being on in Galway," Mary said.

"And you're absolutely certain it was him that gave you this particular fifty euro note?" Fahy said.

"Yes, certain. We sometimes get fellas trying to pass dud fifties in here, so I check every one carefully, and I remember him saying that it was a good note when he saw me examining it. It was him all right," Mary said.

"Right. Thanks for your help, guys. We may need you to make a statement, Mary, but we'll let you know," Mulholland said.

Outside, they agreed that Mulholland should go back to the station while Lyons and Fahy would go down to the hotel and talk to Keogh.

When they got to Dónal's workplace, they asked to see him but didn't say they were police in case his employer might wonder what was going on. As the receptionist went into the kitchen to fetch him, they could hear her say: "Hey Dónal, there are two chicks out front to see you, you bad boy."

Lyons looked at Fahy and giggled. She hadn't been called that before – well, not recently anyway.

Dónal Keogh emerged from the kitchens wearing a pair of black and white chef's pants and a thick white tunic buttoned up to his throat. He was almost six feet tall, thin, with unruly, curly fair hair which looked much too long for a chef. Lyons hoped that he tamed it somehow when he was preparing food.

They introduced themselves, showing their warrant cards, and took him into the lounge which, at that time of the day, was totally empty.

"Dónal, may I ask if you placed a bet in the bookie's here in town the other day with a fifty euro note?" Lyons began.

"Eh, yeah. I did all right. Bloody donkey came in last too. Just my luck."

"Where did you get the fifty euros, Dónal?"

"It was a bit mad really. A bloke bought a drink at the bar with it and told me to keep the change. So, I put the price of his drink in the till myself, and pocketed the fifty, didn't I?"

"What were you doing serving in the bar? I thought you worked in the kitchens," Fahy said.

"I do. But, after I'm finished with the evening meal, they sometimes ask me to work the bar if they're short-handed. I don't mind – the extra money comes in handy," Dónal said.

"And is it normal for someone to tip you that much?" Lyons said.

"Jesus, no. Never happened to me before. It was mad, like. I thought he might have been a foreigner that got mixed up with the money, but he wasn't. He was Irish. Said he was down for the races, and came out here 'cos he couldn't get a room in Galway at a reasonable price."

"Is he staying at the hotel?" Fahy asked.

"No, not here. He didn't say where he was staying, but it must be somewhere in the town, I suppose."

"Is there any CCTV in the bar, Dónal?" Lyons asked.

"No. Nothing like that."

"What did he look like?"

"Just normal. Pretty average. Just an ordinary bloke, quite young too," Dónal said.

"Do you think you could help us to do up a picture of this guy's face, if we got a police artist out here?" Lyons said.

"S'pose so. But I'm no good at drawing myself."

"No, that's fine. Our artist would do the drawing, or he might use a computer to work up an e-fit with you. Would you be around later if we got someone out from Galway?" Lyons said.

"I guess so. Am I in trouble?"

"The fifty euro note that you were given may have been part of a larger sum taken in a robbery, so we need to check everything out very thoroughly, Dónal. Is there any way you can substantiate your story about this very generous stranger?"

"Cripes. I didn't know – honest. But I'm telling the truth, I swear. Ask anyone, I've never stolen anything in my life."

"Is there anything else at all you can tell us about this guy – any little detail? Did he spend any more money at the bar that night?" Fahy asked.

"No. He just had the one pint. He was reading the paper too. The Racing Post, I think, so we didn't talk much."

"Dónal, have you ever heard of a man called John Durnan? He's a bookmaker," Lyons asked.

"No, can't say that I have, Inspector. Who's he?" Keogh said.

Lyons didn't answer the question.

"OK, Dónal. Well, hang around here today till we get the e-fit officer out to you. And if by any chance you see this man again, I want you to let us know immediately. Understood?" Lyons said. She gave him a business card.

"Yeah, OK."

"Just one more thing, Dónal," Fahy said, "where were you on Tuesday afternoon between, say, six o'clock and nine?"

"I was working, wasn't I?"

They let Dónal return to his duties in the kitchen. The lad was obviously bothered by what they had told him.

"What do you reckon, Sally?" Lyons said once they were outside on the pavement again.

"He seems straight enough, boss. I'll see if we have anything on him in the system, just in case. But he doesn't look like a killer to me."

"Me neither, but you're right. Check it out just to be on the safe side. Oh, and have a word with the manager here. Make sure he was actually working at the time of the murder."

Chapter Eleven

The week went on with no further developments for the detectives, which Lyons found particularly frustrating. The races came to an end, the crowds having largely forgotten the fact that there had been a murder at the venue, being totally preoccupied with their own affairs. It takes a lot to dampen the spirit at this particular gathering.

Over the weekend, the masses that had come for the race meeting slowly departed from the hotels, guesthouses, and Airbnb accommodation in the area. The traffic gradually thinned out, and all that was left of the event was a big clean-up job out at Ballybrit, which would start in earnest on the Monday morning.

Further west, out in Connemara proper, the good summer continued to attract large numbers of visitors, brought into the area by the publicity associated with The Wild Atlantic Way. The terrain was mostly heath and bog, and although it looked stunningly beautiful in the midsummer sun, much of the land was unproductive, just about able to sustain a few flocks of scrawny sheep. Since the EU had come down heavily on peat harvesting, introducing legislation to stop the locals from digging out the bog, drying it at the side of the road, and then burning it in their open fires during the long, damp winter months, agricultural activity in the region was at an all-time low.

But here and there, where farmers had put in enormous effort to drain the land and clear it of rocks and stones, a few acres of barley were grown. The crop was used for winter feed for a small number of cattle that would spend several months indoors when the temperature dropped and the strong south-westerly winds blew the moist air in from the Atlantic.

Peadar O'Louhglin brought his huge, pale-green Claas combine harvester to a halt at the gate to one such field of ripe barley early on Tuesday morning. The field was only just over four acres, so he calculated it would take him less than an hour to harvest the grain and be off to the bigger, more lucrative jobs closer to Galway city. He had been cutting this field on behalf of the owner – a now elderly smallholder – for several years, and although he didn't make much from it, he hadn't the heart to stop, as he knew the man would get no other contractor to take on the job. Years ago, the owner himself would have cut the crop down with a scythe, and then his sons would have threshed the stalks to save the grains of barley, and bound up the straw into bails to make bedding for the cattle, or perhaps even to re-thatch the farmhouse. But the man's sons were long gone to America to seek fame and fortune, and he was too old to wield a scythe any longer, and besides, the machine was so quick and efficient, it made sense to employ it.

With the gate opened, Peadar climbed back up into the massive contraption, and manoeuvred it in gingerly through the opening which was barely wide enough to take it. He began cutting down along the ditch that ran alongside the road, and he was on his second swathe when something fouled in the blades of the harvester, causing it to cut out suddenly and jerk to a halt with a loud buzzer sounding in his ears.

"What the blazes?" Peadar grumbled as he climbed back out of the cab and went to the front where the blades had attempted to ingest the obstruction. Making sure that the machine was completely inert, Peadar put his arm into where the debris was lodged, and pulled out what looked to him like an old doctor's bag.

"Well, I'll be damned. What the hell is this doing here?" he said to himself. He stood back from his trusty machine and dusted off the old black bag before opening it to look inside.

"Good God almighty!" he said as he stared into the bag, which was stuffed with hundreds of used banknotes. Peadar looked around to see if anyone had observed him retrieving the bag, but there was no one in sight. He scratched his head for a minute, then closed up the bag again, climbed back into the harvester, and placed the bag securely behind the driver's seat.

* * *

Lyons was at her desk staring blankly at the e-fit that had been produced following a further session with Dónal Keogh. The picture reflected Dónal's appraisal of the man who had given him the large tip – it was just average in every respect, and therefore, Lyons thought, totally useless.

She hated this part of an investigation with a passion. Nothing was happening. There were no further clues to follow up, and she was beginning to think that this one might just slip through her fingers, which made her even more frustrated.

The rest of the team knew her well enough to stay out of her way when she was in this kind of mood. Like Lyons herself, they too were feeling the frustration, but at least they had other crimes, though not as serious, to investigate, and therefore distract them.

Her phone rang to punctuate her gloomy contemplation.

"Lyons."

"Hiya, Maureen. How's things?" Mulholland said.

"Ah, you know. Not great, to be honest, Séan. What can I do for you?"

"Well, this will cheer you up a bit. You'll never guess what I have here on the desk in front of me."

"You're right, Séan, I'll never guess."

"It's only an old doctor's bag that looks just like the one that was on the telly," Mulholland said.

"Wow. Fantastic. Where did you get it?"

"Wait. There's more. Not only have I got the bag, but it's stuffed full of money too. Amazing!"

Mulholland went on to explain that Peadar O'Loughlin had handed in the bag a few minutes ago.

"Christ, Séan, that truly is extraordinary. Do you know the man who handed it in?"

"I do, of course. They're a very good family, and hard-working too. Peadar does a lot of work for charity during the winter when he's not busy with his machinery. He has a special needs son, and he raises a lot of money for them."

"Great. Well, can you wrap it up and get someone to bring it in to Sinéad Loughran? There may be fingerprint evidence we can use. Did you get the man's prints for elimination?" Lyons said.

"Ah now! No, Maureen, I didn't. It would have made it look as if we suspected him of something, and that wouldn't be right. I can get them later if you really need them."

"I see what you mean. OK. Who will you send it in with, so I can tell Sinéad to expect them?"

"I'll get Jim Dolan to drive in with it. He's out on the road at the minute dealing with a stolen horsebox; though, to be honest, I'd say the owner probably just forgot where he left it. But he'll be back in half an hour or so. Will that do ye?"

"Yes. Thanks, Séan. That's fine."

When Lyons had finished the call, she went out into the open plan and told the team about the development.

"But how come the money was still in the bag, boss?" Flynn asked.

"I agree, that's just weird. Of course, we don't know if it's all there, but from what Séan said, it seems there's a good lot of it."

"But that means the motive for the attack wasn't robbery, boss," Sally Fahy said.

"Exactly, Sally – just what I was thinking. Oh, by the way, did anyone interview Ronan, the clerk?" Lyons said.

"Yes, boss. I did. The poor lad was in bits," Flynn said.

"Anything useful to tell us?" Lyons said.

"He just confirmed what we already knew – you know, about the float and stuff. He left before Durnan, and I verified his timings with the lads on the gate. It all checks out. Oh, and Ronan says that Durnan still owed him a monkey for the work he did."

"Well, he can kiss goodbye to that anyway. Do you think he knows anything about the money laundering Hamill was talking about?"

"I doubt it. I didn't broach the subject directly with him. Didn't want to give too much away. But I took the ledger. John is crunching the numbers from it now, but he may need to get a forensic accountant to look at it."

"OK. Well, let me know before we go down that route, will you? We need to keep this tight for the moment."

"Yes, sure, boss."

"Sally, can I have a word in my office?"

* * *

Fahy followed Lyons into her office and they both sat down.

"When that nice man Hamill from Dublin was here, he said that he thought Durnan could have a stash of cash hidden away at the house. If that's the case, then there's two issues we need to look at. Firstly, Mrs Durnan and the girl could be at risk. I've posted a man at the gate of the house to try and offset that one. But – and here's where it gets a bit trickier – I'd like to know if it's true. Is there any chance you could go back out there on some pretext? Go on your own. See if you can get talking to Shauna one to one. Try and get inside her head a bit. If there is a hoard out there, I'd like to get hold of it. It could get us a few brownie points with that bunch of Lotharios up in Dublin," Lyons said.

"I see what you mean. Sure, I'll give it a go. I used to have a pony when I was a teenager anyway, so we'll have something to talk about. Oh, and there's something else, boss. I had a call back just now from the manager of the hotel where Keogh works, out in Clifden. He was away for a few days, but he confirmed that Keogh wasn't working in the hotel on the night Durnan was killed. Apparently, he called in sick that day."

"I see. Interesting. So, Dónal Keogh has no alibi for the time of the murder, and he's been lying to us. I think it's time we had another word with him, don't you? Maybe I'll ask Eamon to go out there and put the fear of God into him – see what emerges."

"Good idea, boss. Shall I ask him to pop in?"

"Yes please, Sally. Thanks."

Chapter Twelve

Jim Dolan arrived during the afternoon with the old Gladstone bag that had been handed in.

"Hi, Jim. Thanks for bringing that in. I love it when a bloke brings me loads of money!" Sinéad Loughran said in her usual cheery way.

"Hi, Sinéad. Where do you want it?"

"Not so fast, tiger. Here, put on these gloves, you're going to have to help me count it. That needs two of us."

"Oh, right. Of course, just in case someone says it's short."

"Exactly. Now, tip it out on the bench here," she said. She gestured towards a wide, clear bench, which is where she spent much of her time analysing samples of one kind or another.

The two of them started by separating out the notes into their various denominations, and making small piles of cash. Then they got to the business of counting, dividing the notes up into thousands. Finally, each counted the other's bundles again, and Loughran made a list on her pad of the running total.

When she was going through the last bundle of twenties, she came across a piece of a Post-it Note stuck to one of the twenties, with some hastily scribbled writing in pencil on it.

"Hey, look at this," she said. She held up the paper scrap.

"I must have missed that. What does it say?" Dolan asked.

"I don't know. Here, have a look – see if you can make it out."

"Let's see. Looks like JD or maybe JB, 2 G 6, or something. Doesn't make any sense to me," Dolan said, and handed back the small morsel of yellow paper to Loughran.

"OK. Well, when we've finished, you'd better let Lyons know. It could be important," he said.

"Will do. So, how much do you reckon we've got in total?" Loughran said.

"I make it twenty-six thousand, four hundred and sixty-five euro exactly."

"Yep, that tallies. Great. Let's put it away before I'm tempted to buy a one-way ticket to Rio," Loughran said.

Dolan looked at her wondering if she was serious for a second.

"Just kidding!"

"Right. Well, if that's me done, I'll be off then," Dolan said.

"Hang on. We both have to sign this evidence form first. Verify the amount. Then I'll get working on the bag. Thanks for your help."

Dolan and Loughran co-signed the form, and he left. Loughran got busy scrutinizing the entire surface of the bag inside and out for fingerprints, or any other traces she could find.

She then phoned Lyons to bring her up to speed.

* * *

"Was there any sign of some new fifty euro notes, possibly still in the bank wrapper?" Lyons asked when Loughran called her.

"No, sorry, Maureen. Nothing like that. There were plenty of fifties, but not new ones, and no wrappers."

"OK, thanks."

When Lyons had finished talking to Sinéad Loughran, she asked John O'Connor to come into her office. She had written down the letters and numbers from the piece of paper on a sheet of her own.

"Hi John, what do you make of this?" She turned her page round so that it faced O'Connor.

O'Connor studied the jottings for a moment.

"Could mean anything, boss. Or nothing. What do you reckon?"

"Same. But now we have the amount of cash that was in the bag, we can do some calculations," she said.

"Sorry, I don't follow you."

"Well, we know from his ledger how much he should have had. So, we can compare it to how much we actually found and see if it tallies."

"Oh, I see what you mean. Give it here and I'll see if I can figure it out. Do you mind if I take it back outside?" O'Connor said.

"Go ahead."

Half an hour later, John O'Connor knocked on Lyons' door.

"Yes, John. What's up?"

"I'm sorry, boss, but I can't make head nor tail of Durnan's ledger, trying to reconcile it against the amount of money in the bag. It doesn't balance, that's for sure."

"Is the money over or under?"

"Look, Inspector, this really isn't my area of expertise. But I'd say the cash is well over, but I could have it all wrong."

"OK, John, don't worry. Tell you what. Ask Eamon to get Ronan, Durnan's clerk, to come in to go through it with you. He'll be able to put you straight. Did you make any headway with the coded thing?"

"No, 'fraid not. Maybe Ronan will be able to decipher it for us."

* * *

Sally Fahy stopped at the gate to Durnan's house to have a quick chat with the Garda on duty. She held up her warrant card, by way of introduction.

"All right, Guard?"

"Yes, thanks Sergeant; all quiet here."

"Anyone in or out?"

"The missus went out about half an hour ago, but the girl is still at home. Do you want me to open the gate for you? They gave me the number."

"No, thanks. I'll ring the bell. I don't want to creep up on her; frighten her to death," Fahy said.

Fahy got out of her car and rang the bell on the gate, which was answered by Shauna Durnan. A moment later, the gates opened slowly and Fahy drove in.

When she got to the house, Shauna was standing in the open doorway. She looked pleased to see another female, albeit a policewoman.

Fahy made the excuse that she just needed to check a few things out, and before long, the two women were chatting away merrily about all sorts. It transpired that Shauna kept two horses – not racehorses – but well-bred animals all the same, so they had something in common to talk about.

When they had had a cup of tea together, Shauna suggested that they go for a walk around the place to have a look at the stables and the other facilities that John Durnan had lovingly provided for his family. The spread was impressive, and Fahy couldn't help being a little bit envious, remembering her own rather modest childhood, and the struggles her father had providing for her own family. Fahy had never had her own stable. Instead, she worked at a local livery and exchanged mucking out and grooming for a few precious hours riding the ponies along the wooded trails.

"This is really fantastic, Shauna. Your dad must have done really well for himself," Fahy prompted as they stroked one of the horses that had come across looking for food when it saw them standing at the railings.

"He did. He knew the business really well, and always seemed to come away from the meetings on the right side," Shauna said.

"Very much on the right side, judging by all this. Was that his only source of income?"

"Yes, of course. Why do you ask?"

Fahy felt that Shauna was sounding a little bit defensive, so she changed tack.

"You did his books for him, didn't you?"

"Yes. They're very straightforward really, once you know what you're doing."

"Did you ever come across anything a bit off in them?"

"No, never. Well, sometimes his bag would be out a couple of hundred euro, but that was when Ronan had forgotten to write in a bet. It gets pretty frantic just before the races start, you know. But generally, the books balanced. I suppose it's in your nature to ask all these questions, Sally."

"Yes, I'm sorry. Force of habit. I'll stop now. What's the other horse called?"

"See – more questions! Just kidding. That one is Darby. He's really sweet."

Fahy kept a close eye out for anywhere that could be used to store large quantities of cash, but she didn't see anything obvious, although it would be simplicity itself to create a secret hiding place in one of the stables.

The two women chatted on for another twenty minutes or so, and then Fahy made her excuses and left.

When Shauna was certain that the detective sergeant was off the premises, she made a phone call.

"Fintan. I've had the law here again. Just snooping. Be careful, I think they suspect something's amiss."

"Thanks, pet."

Chapter Thirteen

"This doesn't make any sense. It's way out," Ronan said. He was sitting beside John O'Connor examining Durnan's ledger.

"Are you sure that the amount from the bag is correct?" he said.

"Yes, certain. It was counted by two separate officers and verified. What's the matter with it?"

"The cash is way over. It's roughly five grand too much. And there's another thing. That last bet for the six o'clock on Monday. I didn't write that in. Look – it's in different writing. This is all wrong."

"Are you sure? Have another look. Maybe you've made a mistake," O'Connor said.

"No, I'm certain. I've been over it twice already. It's definitely all wrong."

"OK. Well, can you write out the discrepancies here on this pad, and make it very clear for us? Thanks."

A few minutes later, John O'Connor came into Lyons' office carrying a piece of paper.

"What's the story, John?"

"Well, it looks as if the bag is about five thousand over what it should be, according to the ledger. It would be more if the float was still there," O'Connor said.

"Hmm, maybe Hamill was right then," Lyons said.

"What's that, boss?"

"Oh, nothing, John. Just daydreaming. Thanks. Make sure the cash is well secured in the evidence room safe, won't you?"

"Yes, boss. Of course."

When O'Connor had left the office, Lyons spent some time staring at the two pieces of paper in front of her. The small scrap that had been found amongst the money, with its secret, coded numbers, and the tally that Ronan and O'Connor had done on the bookie's bag. She instinctively felt that there must be a connection between the two, but couldn't see it.

She was making a copy of both when the phone rang.

"Hi, it's me," Mick Hays said.

"Hi, Mick. What's up?"

"How would you like a nice surprise?" Hays said.

"Oh-oh. Am I going to like this?"

"I hope so. I just had a call from Terence Gillingham out at the Ballynahinch Castle Hotel. He's on the rural crime committee with me. He's had a cancellation for tonight that's all paid up. Double room with dinner and breakfast. He wondered if we'd like to have it. What do you say?"

"Wow! Sounds great. Do you think it's OK to accept it though?" Lyons said.

"Ah, yeah, it will be fine. I'll put it down to a rural crime committee meeting and write it into the book. And it's Friday, don't forget, so we won't have to rush back tomorrow."

"OK, you're on. By the way, does Ballybrit count as 'rural'?"

"Could do – why?"

"That's OK then. Oh, it's nothing much. I have a little puzzle that I'll bring along for you to solve for me. See you soon."

* * *

Ballynahinch Castle is a fine old building that dates from the mid-sixteenth century. It was originally constructed by the O'Flaherty family, a powerful dynasty from the area. Dónal O'Flaherty then married Grace O'Malley – to be known later as "The Pirate Queen of Ireland" – cementing their place as outright rulers of huge tracts of land stretching from Clifden to Moycullen and beyond. Over the years, the castle passed through a number of hands, including Richard Martin who was responsible for proposing the Cruelty to Animals Bill in the House of Commons in the nineteenth century, earning him the nickname "Humanity Dick".

During the famine years in Ireland of 1846 and 1847, the castle provided shelter and sustenance for hundreds of local people.

Later, in the early part of the twentieth century, the property was purchased by an Indian gentleman – His Highness the Maharaja Jam Sahib of Nawanagar. This man had his own private carriage on the Galway to Clifden railway that passed near the castle, until the railway was closed down in 1939. In 1946 the castle passed into the ownership of The Irish Tourist Board and became a hotel.

With its fabulous location, great access to some of the best fisheries in the West of Ireland, a 700 acre partly wooded site, and splendid appointments, the hotel did well, especially from fishing parties from the United Kingdom and Europe. But maintenance costs on these old places are severe, and government funds were scarce in Ireland in the 1950s, so the property was sold on to an American businessman in 1957. Today, it is owned and operated by a highly successful Irish businessman who has poured millions into the property to bring it up to genuine five-star standards. Ballynahinch Castle boasts a long and impressive guest list, including politicians such as Charles de Gaulle, Gerard Ford and his wife Betty, James Callaghan, Prime Minister of Britain, and several well-known celebrities from the entertainment world.

Hays and Lyons arrived at the castle soon after seven o'clock and were met by Gillingham in the lobby.

"Mick, good to see you. And this must be Maureen. You're both very welcome. I've put you in the suite at the top of the house overlooking the lake. I trust you'll find it comfortable."

"That's terrific, Terence. You're very kind. This is a great treat for two hard-working detectives, I can tell you," Hays said.

"Shhh now, Mick. We don't want to frighten the natives! It's just Mr Hays and partner as far as anyone is concerned. None of your Agatha Christie goings-on here!"

They all chuckled, remembering the story of Bertram's Hotel.

"Leave your overnight bags here, I'll have them brought up. May I invite you to a drink after the drive?" Gillingham said.

"Thanks, Terence," Lyons said, "I could murder a gin and tonic."

"Quite!" Gillingham said, noting the irony.

When the two had enjoyed a brace of Hendrick's gin, served with ice and a freshly cut slice of cucumber, Gillingham took them into the dining room, ushering them to a quiet table near the fire which wasn't lit due to the time of year.

"Chef tells me that the trout is particularly good this evening. It was caught on our own lake this afternoon," Gillingham said.

Their host then departed, leaving instructions with the head waiter that their every need was to be accommodated. The resident sommelier came to the table with recommendations for wine to accompany both the starter and the main course, which they gladly accepted.

"I knew there was a reason I fell for you, Mick Hays. I like your friend," Lyons said as their meal got underway.

"There has to be some perks to this job, hun. God knows we see enough of the shittier side of life too. It's nice to appreciate how the more genteel classes eke out a living for themselves."

"Isn't it, though," Lyons replied.

Although Lyons didn't have a very extensive wardrobe, she had a very good dress sense. For their night away, she had donned a light jersey wool dress that was cut off at one shoulder, and had a very smart pale-pink cashmere cardigan over it. Her hair was shiny and hung loosely around her shoulders, and her makeup was subtle, showing off her high cheekbones and big sparkly brown eyes to best advantage.

"It's no surprise I fell for you, Maureen. Just look in the mirror – you look fabulous tonight," Hays responded.

"You old silver-tongued devil, Hays. I know what you're after. You want to see what puzzle I've brought you, don't you?"

They were interrupted by the arrival of their main course. The trout was served with a garlic and lemon butter sauce, sprinkled with fresh herbs. A side dish of steamed baby potatoes and fresh vegetables accompanied it, and the sommelier brought their crisp sauvignon blanc, chilled to just the right temperature, to accompany the meal.

"This is amazing, Mick," Lyons said, "such delicate flavours. And Terence was right, the fish is perfect."

After they had finished their meal and were seated in the lounge having their coffee, Hays said, "There is something I wanted to talk to you about, Maureen."

"Oh, shit. Am I in trouble?"

"No, nothing like that. Remember Sally's pal, Frank Hamill?"

"Yes, of course. Why?"

"Well, after he had gone, I called his boss, Gerry Mulligan. Gerry and I go way back, and I wanted to get my side of the story in first, before Hamill started kicking up a fuss. Actually, I think I might have been a bit hard on him. But, anyway, that's not the point. Gerry told me – strictly off the record – that there's talk of the great and the good establishing a branch of the Serious and Organised Crime Unit in the West. It's all hush hush for now. They don't want word getting out till they are a bit more prepared. Reading between the lines, I'd say Frank Hamill may have been a scout sent here in advance to suss out the lie of the land."

"Terrific. And we sent him off with a flea in his ear – actually, both ears."

"I think that actually may play to our advantage. We showed we were a joined-up team looking out for one another and not prepared to tolerate any shite. That's what SOCU is all about. They get into some pretty tight spots, and they have to watch each other's backs all the time. Kinda like the SAS of the Gardaí if you will."

"Hmm, I see. Can you get any more from this Gerry fella?"

"Sure. He said he'll square Frank off in any case, but from the way he was talking, I'd say we'll be hearing more about it. Watch this space. Now, what's your puzzle?"

Lyons took the small page from her jotter with the code they had found in amongst Durnan's cash, and showed it to her partner.

Hays studied it for a couple of minutes.

"Can I phone a friend?" he said.

"Hmm. I couldn't figure it out either. Never mind. It'll keep."

Chapter Fourteen

Hays and Lyons left Ballynahinch Castle soon after ten the following morning. It was another bright day, but there was quite a stiff westerly breeze, although the castle was well-sheltered from the worst of it by virtue of its position.

They had spent a very comfortable and intimate night in the magnificent four-poster bed, and had eaten a hearty breakfast before departing. There was no sign of Terence Gillingham, so they resolved to write him a thank-you letter when they arrived home.

"What's your man Gillingham like, anyway?" Lyons said as they drove down the long track leading to the road.

"He's very nice. He doesn't know much about crime or how to deal with it, but he's keen to show willing and support the local community. It's a long tradition to do with the property. They have always helped out the folks around and about whatever way they can, and he's keen to continue it. He does a lot more as well, supporting some of the poorer families in the area and some of the old timers that are living alone, but keeps it very low-key. I like him."

"Cool. Yes, I think I read somewhere that the Castle looked after a good few of the locals during the potato famine. Allowed them to fish the lakes, and hunt game on the land. But listen, Mick, do you mind if we don't go straight home?"

"No, course not. Where do you want to go?"

"I know this is a bit crazy, but I have a hunch."

"Oh-oh. Someone's in trouble. Go on," Hays said.

"No, it's just that one of the cleaners out at the racecourse said that he might have seen a grey Volkswagen van parked in a funny position the night Durnan was killed. He noticed it because it had yellow number plates, and it just looked a bit out of place."

"So?"

"Well, the fifty euro note from Durnan's float turned up out in Clifden. I was just thinking."

"Right. So where to then?"

"Head out towards Roundstone. Let's pay a courtesy call on our old friend Tadgh Deasy. I know it's a long shot, but you never know."

"Christ, Maureen. There are long shots and long shots. Are you sure?"

"Humour me, Mick. And it's a nice day for a drive anyway."

They drove out along the N341, flanked by the sparkling river waters that provided such good trout fishing in season, and on to The Anglers' Rest where the road split – the left-hand section going on towards Cashel, and the right-hand turn that would take them into Roundstone. When they had negotiated the narrow, twisty section, the road rose up onto the heathland, where they could clearly see the Twelve Bens in the distance, looking majestic in their "Paul Henry Blue".

* * *

Hays pulled his Mercedes into the grimy yard where Tadgh Deasy and his son Shay plied their dodgy trade. All around the yard, old and rotting corpses of cars that were being dismantled or simply decaying silently into the earth stood, some piled two and three high, making precarious towers of rusting steel.

There were a couple of slightly fresher looking vehicles too. A Nissan Almera with a piece of white paper stuck in the windscreen offering it for sale at a bargain price of €2,200 "or nearest offer" sat beside a pale-blue Ford Focus bearing a similar advertisement boasting "low mileage" and "only 3 previous owners", as if this in some way added to the value of it.

The two detectives got out of the car and were met by Deasy himself who emerged from a large, dark, corrugated iron shed where he had clearly been working on something very oily.

"Ah, hello Inspector Lyons. How are you doing? And who's this you have with you?"

Lyons introduced Hays, who declined to shake hands with Deasy for obvious reasons.

"God, I'm honoured. Two of Galway's finest to see me in the one day. What can I do for you?"

Lyons had broken off, and was walking around the yard snooping here and there and looking to see if she could find anything of interest while Hays engaged Deasy in conversation.

"We were just out this way for a drive, Tadgh, and we thought we'd pay a social call. How are things?"

Deasy was uneasily watching where Lyons was going.

"Fair to middling. You know yourself, Superintendent."

Lyons went to the side of the workshop and disappeared. A moment later, she was back.

"You have a nice-looking grey VW van around the side there, Tadgh, with no number plates on it. What's the story?"

"I'm giving it a bit of a clean-up. She just came in the other day. I have a bit of work to do on her and then she'll be ready for sale, or I might decide to keep it myself."

"And where are the registration plates?" Lyons said.

"Ah, they're around here somewhere. I took them off to clean behind them."

"Very thorough, Tadgh. But I need to see them. Could you get them for me, please?"

Deasy said nothing, but slouched off back into the darkness of the workshop. They could hear him rooting around inside. A minute later, he emerged holding two oblong registration plates with a recent Dublin number on them. The two plates even matched.

"Now, are you sure they are from the Volkswagen van, Tadgh? You see, I've taken a photograph of the VIN number from the windscreen, and as soon as I get to a Garda station, I'll be checking it out, and I wouldn't like to find that they don't pair up."

"Ah, feck yez," Deasy said under his breath, and walked off back into the abyss of the shed.

He was back a few minutes later with two shiny yellow plastic number plates.

"Here ye are," he said, thrusting them forward for Hays to take.

Lyons photographed the numbers on her iPhone.

"So, where did you get the van, Tadgh? Who brought it in?"

"Just some punter. Said he couldn't be arsed re-registering it and paying the VRT and all. Anyway, he wanted something smaller. So, he traded it for a nice little Ford van I had here."

"And I presume he gave you all the paperwork for the VW?"

"He said he didn't have it with him. He's going to drop it in to me one of the days."

"Jesus, Tadgh. This is way beyond your usual slightly iffy deals. I'm not sure we're going to be able to let this one pass," Lyons said.

"Give me a break, will ye? Shay has to go into hospital again, and I need to get some readies quick to pay for it. And I haven't done anything illegal anyway," Deasy said.

"Maybe not yet, you haven't. But you were going to, weren't you? I bet in a few days that van would be out front here, looking good with a nice set of Irish plates and paperwork to match, for sale for a handy sum. Anyway, I need a description of the man who brought it in, and I'll have to get forensics out here to go over it – that is if you haven't wiped away anything useful there might have been in it. Don't touch it for now, and don't move it – OK?"

"Just my bleeding luck. Right."

Lyons walked away out of earshot and called Sinéad Loughran on her mobile phone.

"Hi, Sinéad. Sorry to disturb you on a Saturday, but we need someone out at Deasy's garage near Roundstone to go over a grey VW van he has here. We think it might be connected to the Durnan killing. Could you get someone for us?"

"Hi, Maureen. Sure, I might as well come on out myself. I was only going to the hairdresser's anyway, and that can wait. I'll get Paul to come with me. What are you looking for, exactly?"

"Ah, you know – the usual. Fingerprints; fibres from clothing; traces from the tyres that might place it at the racetrack; and anything else you can find. But we don't want to have to wait here till you drive out, so I'll get Pascal Brosnan to come and babysit the van till you get here."

"OK. Are you around later in case we find anything?" Loughran said.

"Yes, sure. Give me a call one way or the other. Thanks."

Lyons then called Pascal Brosnan. Brosnan ran the Garda station in Roundstone with the help of another female officer, Mary Fallon. It was usually quiet enough, acting more as a deterrent against wrongdoing than anything else. But over the past few years it had been surprisingly busy, and any talk of closing it down was now abandoned, as the fortunes of the Gardaí improved with the recession now well behind them.

Brosnan arrived at Deasy's yard some fifteen minutes later, and Hays and Lyons handed over their watch, making sure that Deasy couldn't interfere with the VW until the forensic team arrived.

Lyons instructed the young officer to tell Deasy that the van was now police evidence, and that if he so much as breathed on it before they were completely finished with it, he'd be in even more trouble than he was already.

Before Hays and herself drove away, she said to Brosnan, "And get the full details of the vehicle the guy who traded in the grey van bought. Then put out an all-points bulletin for it. It could well be that the driver is the man who killed John Durnan."

As they set off, Hays said, "Honest to God, Maureen, you and your hunches! How the hell do you do it?"

"It's my superpower, Mick. Everybody has one, and we know what yours is!"

Hays slapped her affectionately on the leg and they both laughed.

Chapter Fifteen

Eamon Flynn was feeling decidedly grumpy as he drove
out along the N59 towards Clifden. He had had a late
night the previous evening and imbibed rather too much
alcohol, which didn't improve his humour. He didn't
object to working weekends, but felt this might be more of
a wild goose chase than anything else, so he wasn't best
pleased.

He had arranged for two of Séan Mulholland's men to
bring Dónal Keogh to the Garda station in Clifden. He
had a room in the staff quarters at the hotel where he
worked, so it was easy enough to find him. Keogh was
very curious, and not a little nervous, when the two
uniformed officers turned up and demanded that he
accompany them to the station for questioning in
connection with John Durnan's murder.

"Good morning, Séan," Flynn said to Sergeant
Mulholland as he entered the station.

"Ah, good morning, Inspector. We have your man here in the interview room. Would you like a cup of tea before you start the interview? I have the kettle just boiled."

"Thanks, Seán. Yes please, and have you a biscuit to go with it? I didn't get time for breakfast this morning."

"I can send Peadar out to get you a breakfast roll if you like? They do a fairly good one in the café just a few doors down."

"God, that would be great. Thanks a million," Flynn said, handing over a ten euro note.

Feeling better having devoured his breakfast and drunk several cups of Mulholland's sugary tea, Flynn made his way to the interview room where Dónal Keogh was seated uneasily at the Formica-topped table. A uniformed Garda was standing inside the door.

Flynn nodded to the Garda, and he departed, leaving the inspector alone with the suspect.

"Now, Dónal, is it? Have you any idea why you're here?" he began.

"I dunno. Must be something to do with that fifty euro note, I guess, but I told the other lot all about that."

"Except that you lied about it, didn't you?"

"No, I never. Honest. I told them. I got it as a tip from a geezer in the hotel bar."

"And do you often get fifty-euro tips, Dónal?"

"No, course not. He must've had a big win or something. I dunno."

"Or maybe you hit the jackpot when you whacked Durnan over the head. Why don't you tell me what happened?"

"What do ye mean? I didn't whack anyone over the head. You're making this up!"

"Oh, I can promise you, I'm not. John Durnan is definitely dead, and you just happened to have a fifty euro note that was taken from his bag about your person. And you lied to us about your whereabouts on the night in question. So, you can see how it looks, can't you?" Flynn said.

"I never. I told your lot that I was working, didn't I?" Keogh said. He was perspiring now.

"Yes, you did. But when we checked with the hotel, they said you had called in sick. So, you weren't working, were you?"

Keogh looked down at the floor and muttered something under his breath.

"Well?" Flynn said. He was becoming impatient with this man.

"No, I was working. Just not at the hotel."

"Where then?" Flynn said.

"Jesus, this looks awful. At the bloody races, that's where."

"I see. So, you're telling me you were actually at the Galway Racecourse, allegedly working, the night John Durnan was killed?"

"A mate of mine is well in with the people who run the bars for the races, and they were short-handed. He called me at around noon and asked me if I could come in and do a shift. There'd be good money if I could help out – cash in hand, like. And he said the tips were great too, so I called in sick and got the bus to Galway. I was working the bar from about half two till it closed at nine. And that's the truth."

"Where did you get the brick?" Flynn asked.

"What brick? What are you talking about?" Keogh said.

"Never mind. So, this mate of yours. What's his name and where can I contact him to verify your story?"

"I dunno. He moves around a lot. He could be anywhere by now. He goes to loads of festivals and outdoor things over the summer."

Flynn leaned in towards Dónal Keogh and said softly, "Listen, pal. You're not helping yourself much. Looks to me like we have motive and opportunity here, and it won't be long before we find some link between you and the murder weapon, trust me. If you don't fancy doing life in Mountjoy, you'd better start talking before I run out of patience and charge you with murder. Now, give me something I can work with."

"Look, I dunno. Maybe there was CCTV in the bar at the racecourse that will show me working there right through. I didn't do it. I'm telling the truth."

"Well, at least give me your mate's mobile number, so I can check that part of your story out."

"Fuck it. I don't have it. He called me at the hotel, and I lost my mobile with all my contacts in it last month. Sorry."

"You're the one who'll be sorry. You'll have to stay here till I see if I can find out what you have actually been up to." Flynn got up and left the room, asking the uniformed officer to return to keep Keogh company. When he got back to the main office, he called Lyons and told her what Keogh had said.

"Crikey. Looks like we may have our man. But I'm not sure. It all seems a bit too easy to me. What do you think?" Lyons said.

"I agree. I'll get on to that manager guy out at the racecourse on Monday and see if they have CCTV from the bar anyway. What'll I do with your man?"

"Let him stew for a few hours. It won't do him any harm. Then bail him. We won't be able to do anything much over the weekend anyway. Have you heard anything from Sinéad?"

"No. I'll give her a call when we're finished and maybe drop in to her on the way back to town if she's still at Deasy's."

"OK. Cool. Talk later."

Sinéad Loughran was indeed still at Deasy's yard when Flynn called her.

"I've found a few useful things here in that van," she said.

"Like what?" Flynn said.

"Drop in as you're passing and I'll tell you when I see ya!" She hung up.

Flynn was feeling even more frustrated now. He told Séan Mulholland what to do with Dónal Keogh, and left the Garda station in Clifden. The drive back through Ballyconneely and Roundstone had a soothing effect on him. The weather was still very fine, and the scenery was breathtaking all along the coast, with the Atlantic waves lapping gently on the golden sand in the various small inlets along the way. Even when the road turned inland, the sun glistening on the rocky terrain with the heather just starting to come into bloom made a stunning sight. By the time he reached Deasy's yard, two kilometres past Roundstone, he had calmed down considerably.

"Hi, Sinéad. What's a nice girl like you doing in a place like this?"

"Hi, Eamon. Come with me, young man, and I'll show you something to cheer you up!"

Sinéad led Flynn around to where the VW van was standing with all its doors open. Several evidence bags were lying on the floor.

"What have we got?" Flynn said.

"I found a receipt under the floor mat. Looks like it's for a fill of diesel. It's from that big gas station just off the M6 in Athlone, and it's from the day of the murder."

"Nice. Anything else?"

"Patience, Inspector, patience. Don't deny me my big reveal!"

Flynn smiled.

Loughran went around to the large side door of the van, reached in, and pulled out a large brown paper bag with a plastic window along its length.

"Bricks. Three in all, and they look just like the one we found at the murder site. Of course, I'll have to check when I get this lot back to the lab. But I'm guessing they're from the same batch."

"OK. Good work, Sinéad, that's terrific," Flynn said.

Loughran turned to face Flynn and gave a little curtsy before getting on with the examination of the vehicle.

"I'm just going to have a word with our Mr Deasy. Cheers," Flynn said.

Chapter Sixteen

Lyons was in early on Monday morning. She had enjoyed a pleasant day on Sunday down at the sailing club with Mick, messing about on his boat. They hadn't actually taken it out. There was a stiff breeze, and Lyons was inclined to get seasick, but there's always something to be done on sailing boats, and the fresh sea air gave them a good appetite which they sated later in one of their favourite restaurants further up along the Atlantic coast.

The day had taken her mind off the current case, but only to a limited extent. She was silently processing all the evidence – such as it was – that they had gathered on the murdered bookmaker, and slowly formulating a plan for the week ahead. Hays knew better than to challenge her on the slightly distant manner that he noticed at times during the day, but on the way home, he broached the subject gingerly with her.

"Have you thought of anything more in the Durnan case?"

"Sorry, I hope I wasn't too preoccupied."

"No, you're grand. I know the way your mind works, and I wouldn't try to interfere with that process. It would be more than my life is worth!"

"God. Am I that bad?"

"'course not. I know better than anyone that this isn't a nine-to-five job. But if you want to run any theories past me, feel free."

"Nah. It's OK. I've parked it for now. Anyway, I have other things on my mind," she said, moving closer to him in the car and putting her hand on his thigh.

* * *

When Lyons called the team together just after half past eight the following morning, she had her thoughts well organised.

"OK. Listen up everyone. Busy day ahead."

Flynn, Fahy and O'Connor shuffled into their seats. Flynn had a takeaway coffee in his hand which Sally Fahy was eyeing enviously.

"OK. Let's start with everything we've got so far. Eamon, you first."

Flynn described the interview that he had conducted with Dónal Keogh out in Clifden, and reported that he had asked Séan Mulholland to get one of his men to keep an eye on the lad.

"Are we tailing him around?" Fahy asked.

"No. Just clocking his movements in and out of work, that sort of thing. Seeing if he has any more ready cash that isn't obviously accounted for. Meanwhile, I've asked John to have a deep dive into our system and see if we have anything at all on him."

"Anything so far, John?" Lyons asked.

"No, boss. Not a trace."

"OK, Eamon, what else?"

"Well, there's the grey van we found out at Deasy's. That looks a bit more promising. John, tell us what you've found."

"Well, the plates belong to a Ford Mondeo that was written off in the UK a few months back. The report says a container fell on it. Luckily, it was parked and empty at the time, but it was scrapped. Then I looked up the VIN number for the van. The latest we can find is that it was sold at auction along with four other vehicles to a Brendan Moran. Moran runs a second-hand dealership out on the Tuam Road, and he's known to us," O'Connor said.

"Oh, how's that?" Lyons asked.

Flynn interjected, "We think he may be money laundering for someone. We haven't managed to nail him yet, but his turnover is crazy, as are his prices – far too cheap to be legit."

"Right, so there could be an organised crime connection after all, then. Terrific! That's all we bloody need," Lyons said.

"Do you think we should pay Mr Moran a visit, boss?" Sally Fahy asked.

"He'll keep for now, Sally. I'd better check it with Mick in case SOCU have something going on with him. We've already blotted our copy book in that department, and I don't want to make it worse. What about the Durnan family – anything there?"

"Not much. Shauna went off on Saturday towing an empty horsebox, and came back about an hour and a half later with it loaded with sacks of animal feed. Our lad at the gate said there were about twenty bags of the stuff in the trailer. Apart from that, just the occasional visitor. We have the details, but there's nothing suspicious," Fahy said.

"OK. So – plans for the day. John, can you start looking into Durnan's bank account. See if you can spot anything out of the ordinary. Sally, I want you to follow up on the receipt Sinéad found in the van. Get onto the petrol station that issued it and see if they have any CCTV or anything. If necessary, go out there and have a look around. Eamon, will you find out where Shauna Durnan buys her horse feed? I'd like to know how she paid for it. That stuff isn't cheap. Let's reconvene mid-afternoon," Lyons said.

"What are you going to get up to, boss?" Flynn asked.

"I'm going to follow up this Brendan Moran thing a bit – see what's going on. And when the hour gets decent, I'll give Sinéad a call and see what she's found out about the bricks in the van."

* * *

Back in her office, Lyons called Mick Hays.

"Hi, Mick. Have you got a sec?"

"Sure. What's up?"

Lyons explained about the van, and its connection to Brendan Moran Motors on the Tuam Road.

"Do you think we need to talk to SOCU before going in with our size nines and getting into more trouble?" Lyons said.

"Probably a good idea. I'll give Gerry Mulligan a call and see what the story is. Where's the van now?"

"It's still out at Deasy's yard."

"Well, it might be a good idea to collect it. What do you think?" Hays said.

"Yeah, you're right. Best not to drive it, though. I'll organise a low-loader. Let me know what gives with Superintendent Mulligan. If we're going to give Moran a rattle, I'll need a warrant as well."

"That's no problem, but wait till I get back to you. OK?"

"Yeah, sure. Thanks, Mick."

* * *

Hays wasted no time in making the call to his pal in Dublin. He knew Lyons wouldn't want to hang about, and if there was some organised crime connection, the sooner it was tackled, the better.

"Hi, Gerry. It's Mick Hays again."

Hays went on to explain the reason for the call.

"OK, Mick. Would you be happy if we sent someone down to you? And before you ask, it won't be Hamill."

"Ah. How is the lovely Frank these days, anyway?"

"I've moved him onto people trafficking. He's still smarting from that little trick you pulled on him with the speed trap, but he'll get over it. Anyway, we have a lassie here who's getting stuck into the money laundering thing in a big way now. I'm sure she'd enjoy a trip out West, and obviously a female officer would be less of a concern given what you told me about Frank."

"Sounds good, Gerry. What is the lady's name?"

"Inspector Valerie White. Very ambitious, and easy on the eye too. Keen as mustard to get on. She's a rising star here, so look after her well for me."

"Oh, don't worry, we will. Thanks, Gerry. Ask her to liaise with Senior Inspector Maureen Lyons," Hays said. He gave Mulligan Maureen's details.

Chapter Seventeen

Inspector Eamon Flynn covered the distance to Nutfield Cross on the edge of Ballinasloe in under forty-five minutes. As he approached the Durnan residence, he noticed that there was no sign of the Garda who should have been stationed outside on the road. He did spot a pale-blue Ford Mondeo parked up against the ditch near the gates to the property, but it was unoccupied.

He got out of the car and pressed the buzzer that was mounted on the pillar, announcing his arrival to Mrs Durnan who had answered the bell. A moment later, the gates started to open slowly, and he drove in. As he approached the building, a uniformed Garda in a high-vis jacket emerged from around the side of the house, putting his uniform cap back on.

Flynn hopped out of the car as the young man set off down the drive.

"Hold on there a moment, Guard. We need a word," Flynn said.

The young Garda turned back to where Flynn was now standing outside the house on the gravel driveway.

"I'm Inspector Eamon Flynn from Galway. What's your name, Guard?" Flynn said.

"Garda Whelan, sir; Ultan Whelan."

"Why aren't you at your post at the gate?"

Garda Whelan indicated he wanted to have a quiet word with the inspector well out of earshot of the house. The two men walked a little way down the drive, and the young officer started to speak.

"I'm getting on well with the family, sir. They ask me in for a cup of tea around this time in the morning, and I'm taking the opportunity to find out a good bit about them and how they operate."

"I hope you've got something useful to report. You were told to stay at the gates."

Whelan looked a bit uneasy, and turned Flynn away from the house. He spoke softly.

"I might have, sir. There was a guy here on Saturday, an electrician. It seems he had done a lot of work out the back around the stables putting in some new lights and a few extra power points."

"So, what's odd about that?"

"Well, when I was having a cuppa in the kitchen, this guy presented his bill. There was a bit of talk about VAT. It was something like seven hundred euro, without the tax. When they settled on an amount, Shauna disappeared for a few minutes and came back with a fistful of cash and gave it to the electrician."

"Where did she go to get the money?"

"I'm not sure, but there were a few bits of hay mixed up with it, so she may have got it in the stables somewhere. At least, that's what I thought," Whelan said.

"And who have you reported this to, Ultan?"

"Eh, I haven't had a chance, sir. I was going to call it in when I got back to the car just now."

"OK. Well, don't bother with that. You've told me. I'm not sure how Senior Inspector Lyons will take your bit of detective work, but it may be useful. Just don't overdo it. If anything happens here and you're not at your post, you'll be spending the rest of your career on the Aran Islands."

"Thanks, sir. I'll be getting on then." Whelan walked down the rest of the driveway and resumed his sentry duty at the gate.

Jessica Durnan welcomed Flynn and offered him tea, which he declined. She was in much better form than the last time he had seen her, and Flynn had to admit that she was a fine-looking woman. He gave her a little bit of information about how the investigation was going, without saying too much. He asked where Shauna was, and Mrs Durnan said that she was probably either in the stables or out in the paddock with one of the horses.

"If it's OK with you, I'll just catch up with her and tell her how things are going," Flynn said.

"Yes, all right, Inspector. But before you go, can I ask if there's any news on when we may be able to bury my husband?" Mrs Durnan said.

"I'm sorry, Mrs Durnan, but it could be a little while yet, I'm afraid. I'll have a word back at the station and see if I can get any more accurate information for you."

"Thanks, Inspector. Can I leave you to find Shauna outside? I have some phone calls to make."

"Yes, yes, of course. I'll be in touch."

Flynn let himself out through the back door and strolled around to the stable block. He found Shauna unloading the horsebox, carrying the 25Kg bags of animal feed into a small, dark storeroom.

"Here, let me take some of those for you," Flynn said.

"It's OK. I can manage. I'm used to it," she said.

Flynn ignored Shauna's refusal of help and lifted a bag out of the back of the trailer and followed her into the dry store, stacking the bag on top of the others neatly.

"You must get through a lot of this stuff," he said.

"Tell me about it. It disappears in no time."

"Where do you buy it?" Flynn said.

"The Co-op in Athenry. It's a bit of a distance to go for it, but the horses like this brand, and their prices are very good."

Flynn lifted the last bag out of the trailer and walked back indoors alongside Shauna.

"How much does it cost anyway?" he said.

"These are twenty-three euros each. But if I buy twenty bags at a time, they give them to me for twenty-one."

"Wow. Expensive business, keeping horses."

"Yeah, I guess, but they're worth it. And Dad was very generous. He loved horses," Shauna said, welling up with the memory of her dead father.

"I'm sorry, Shauna. I know this is hard. I promise, we're doing our very best to find out who did this. We will find him, it's just a matter of time."

"I know," she said, blowing her nose in a tissue, "but it won't bring him back, will it?"

"No, it won't. But it will give you some closure, trust me," Flynn said.

There was little more that Flynn could do to comfort the distraught girl, so he made his excuses, checking that Shauna wasn't too distressed, and left.

When he got to the gate, he had another word with Garda Whelan through the open window of his car.

"Ultan, if you get a chance, see if you can find out where this lot are stashing their cash, but don't get caught snooping around. If you find anything, call me at once, OK?" Flynn said.

"Yes, sir, of course."

Flynn turned left out the gate, towards Athenry.

* * *

When Lyons had finished talking to Hays, she called the motor pool and arranged for a tow truck to go out to Deasy's yard and collect the grey VW van. She then rang Pascal Brosnan in Roundstone and asked him to go to Tadgh Deasy's place as well to ensure that there was no attempt to prevent the removal of the van, or interfere with it, before the Gardaí could get their hands on it.

"And while you're there, Pascal, tell our friend Deasy that he's not out of the woods on this one. I'm not finished with him yet."

"Are you going to charge him, Inspector?" Brosnan said.

"Let's see how this thing all works out, Pascal. We may have our hands full without having to deal with the likes of him. But don't let on. I want him thinking he's in right trouble. We'll get more out of him that way," Lyons said.

"Right, so. Don't worry, Inspector, I'll look after it."

"Good man, Pascal. Catch you later."

Lyons went and got herself a coffee, and when she was back at her desk, she called Sinéad Loughran.

"Hi, Sinéad. Have you had a chance to look at the bricks we got back from the van?" Lyons asked.

"Hi, Maureen. Yes, and as suspected, they are a match to the one that was used to whack Durnan over the head. But there's more. We recovered a few stubs from small cigars from the ashtray too. I've sent them off to Dublin to see if they can get any DNA traces from them. My equipment here isn't up to it, I'm afraid. And we got a partial fingerprint from the back of the driver's door handle. Deasy isn't exactly a star performer when it comes to valeting cars!"

"Cool. That's great. Do we have a match from the print?"

"No. It's not enough for us to match here, so it's gone to Dublin too. Do you think you could have a word with the Superintendent about getting us some better equipment next time he's doing his budgets? It's a pain having to send all this stuff up to Dublin all the time," Loughran said.

"I doubt if he'd listen to me on that one, Sinéad. His blessed budgets are one of the mysteries of the modern world, but I'll put in a word when I get him in the humour."

"I was thinking, you could always withhold certain privileges to persuade him - you know."

"Jesus, girl! No chance. We make it a rule never to bring work inside the house, but I could mention it to him all the same – just not at home."

"And there was me thinking you two solved all these dastardly murders while you were snuggled up in bed together."

"You need to get out more, Sinéad."

The two of them laughed.

"So, when will you have the results back from the lab?" Lyons said.

"Probably a day or two. I'll start pestering them tomorrow afternoon. Then they'll ask me if I have any idea how many samples they have to process ahead of mine, so I'll put on my little-girl-lost routine, and I'll get them to bump them up the queue."

"God. You're incorrigible! Let me know as soon as you have anything," Lyons said.

"Sure, no problem. See ya."

Chapter Eighteen

Sally Fahy was feeling impatient. It should have taken her just over an hour to get from Mill Street to the petrol station outside Athlone, but she put on the blue lights in the white Hyundai Garda car, and used the sirens liberally to cut through the mid-morning traffic. Once on the M6, she brought the squad car up to 160kph, and flew past anything that appeared in front of her.

Fahy had completed the Garda's advanced driving course, and the road was dry, although ominous grey clouds hung in the overhead sky, threatening rain which never actually arrived. She knew the car was fairly new, and well maintained, so she had no hesitation in booting it along at what would normally be much too fast for her driving style.

As she approached the petrol station, she turned off the blue lights and slowed down, pulling sedately into the car park in front of the sprawling array of fuel pumps and the enormous glass fronted shop and café.

Inside, she bought a much-needed coffee, produced her warrant card, and asked to see the manager. While the assistant went off to seek out her boss, Fahy sat at one of the tables covered in the detritus of someone's earlier breakfast, and waited.

After a minute or two, a short, plump bespectacled woman wearing a navy trouser suit approached.

"Sergeant Fahy," she said, holding out a pudgy hand for Sally to shake, "my name is Gretta. I'm the manager here today. How can I help?"

Fahy explained the reason for her visit, and asked Gretta to retrieve any CCTV footage that they might have from the date imprinted on the receipt recovered from the VW van. Helpfully, the receipt was also time-stamped, which made the task a lot easier.

"We should have that in the office. We keep them for a month for security reasons. You have no idea how many drivers we get who fill up their cars and drive off without paying. But we usually nail them in the end. The cameras are a godsend. Would you like to come with me to the office, or, if you prefer, I can get the CD, and you can stay here and finish your coffee?" Gretta said.

"I'll come with you, if that's OK?" Fahy said, standing up.

On the way through the back of the working area in the busy café, Fahy asked Gretta if they ever prosecuted the fuel thieves.

"We usually tell them if they pay the full amount, we won't report it. That nearly always works. We have a 94% recovery rate," Gretta said.

"That's a very precise figure, Gretta."

"I know. The company gets a monthly report on theft and recovery rates. They classify it as spillage, but it isn't, of course. They don't like to admit how easy it is to rip us off. I wish we had pre-pay like they do in the States. That would stop it completely. You know, almost half a cent in every litre goes on spillage. And that's a lot when you consider we only have a margin of around seven cents to start with," the woman said.

They reached the office, which was small and packed with files, computers, and various bits and pieces that had been brought in from the shop with spoiled packaging. Although it was clearly a busy place, it was by no means chaotic, and Fahy was surprised at how orderly the filing system was that allowed Gretta to retrieve the relevant recording from the cabinet in a couple of seconds.

"Here you go," she said, offering Fahy a CD in a plastic sleeve with the date written on it in black felt pen.

"Thanks. Do you need to make a copy, or is it OK to take this one away?"

"No, take it. I'll put a note in the file. Do you want to look at it here?" Gretta asked.

"No, it's OK. I'll take it back to our tech guy in Galway. He'll get the information we want from it. Here's my details. You can contact me if you need it back," Fahy said, and handed Gretta a card.

"If you'd like to get something to eat before you head back, or if you need to take a drink to have in the car, please just select whatever you want – on us. Oh, and let us know how you get on with your case. I hope it works out for you, whatever it is."

"Thanks very much. I'm fine for food and drink, but thanks anyway. I'll call you if there are any developments," Fahy said.

Fahy drove at a less frantic pace back to Galway. She was more relaxed now that she had the CCTV footage in her possession. She kept to the speed limit, and slowed down even more as she approached the city, the summer rain having started to fall, making the roads slick and greasy. To make the point, she passed an accident on one of the roundabouts where a bus had slid into the back of a lorry. Uniformed Gardaí were in attendance.

* * *

Back at the station, Fahy gave the CD to John O'Connor.

"Here you go, John. And the receipt is timed at 14:34, so it should be easy enough to pick out our hero," Fahy said.

"Hmm. The time stamps on those things are usually very inaccurate, but it will give us an idea, at least. Why don't you stay and watch the show?"

"OK. It'll be better than the shite that's on TV at the moment anyway."

"Let's hope," O'Connor said. He loaded the disc into one of his several computers.

They watched as the screen filled with an image divided into three segments. On the left there was a long view of the pumps that occupied half the screen, and then on the right the image was divided horizontally in two. The top half showed the shop, and the lower half the tills where customers paid for their purchases.

O'Connor fast-forwarded the film to 14:25 using the timeline imprinted on the foot of the image, and then slowed it down to normal speed.

At 14:28 the grey VW van pulled in and stopped at one of the diesel pumps. A thin young man got out, and went about filling the van with fuel. He was dressed in blue jeans, a t-shirt, and annoyingly, a baseball cap which largely hid his face from the camera. But when he went inside to pay, the camera at the till had recorded a much better image of the man, and his face was clearly visible for almost twenty seconds. Fahy noted that he paid in cash, and bought a Lotto scratchcard with some of the change.

"Bingo! That could very well be our man, John. Nice one," Fahy said.

"John, can you print off some stills from that bit with the image of this guy's face. And can you get it into the database, and see if he's known to us?"

"Sure, no problem. How many stills do you want?"

"Just four or five for now. Enough for the afternoon briefing. Let's see how Inspector Lyons wants to play it. Thanks."

* * *

Inspector Flynn arrived at the Co-op on the outskirts of Athenry. It was a large sprawling complex, with all sorts of colourful farm machinery parked outside a vast dark-green steel shed. There was an enormous plate glass window set into the front of the building, and in it there were many advertisements for that month's special deals on pig feed; chicken feed; fertilizer of all kinds; and even discounted farm implements.

Flynn parked up beside a large Toyota pick-up truck covered in mud and went into the shop. Inside, on the right-hand wall, there was a noticeboard carrying more advertisements, this time for contractors and some second-hand equipment that members of the organisation had for sale. Further in, over to the left-hand side of the huge premises, there was a counter manned by five men, each perched on chairs with PC screens in front of them. Flynn approached the first man who wasn't serving a customer and introduced himself.

"I was wondering if you know a girl by the name of Shauna Durnan? She buys horse feed here from time to time," Flynn said. He showed his warrant card to the man.

The man turned to the chap on his left.

"Hey, Jimmy, that girl that comes in here for horse feed, and always asks for you. You know the one you dream about every night – long brown hair, nice figure – she's a Durnan, isn't she?"

"Yep," Jimmy replied proudly, "that's my Shauna, and she calls me Jimmy."

"In your dreams, you pervert," the man in front of Flynn said, addressing his colleague.

Flynn edged across so that he was now standing in front of Jimmy.

"When was Shauna last in?" Flynn asked.

"Just this week. She bought 20 bags of premium balancer, so I gave her a few quid off. But it won't last long – she'll be back to see me soon enough," Jimmy said with a smile, relishing the thought.

"Right, Jimmy, can I ask how she paid?" Flynn said.

"Oh, cash – always cash with Shauna. No messing with credit there. She's not just cute – she's loaded."

"So, it's her money you're after, you dirty bugger," the man seated beside Jimmy said.

"Feck off, Tommy. You're just jealous," Jimmy said, and the two men laughed.

"How often does Shauna come in for feed?" Flynn said.

"About every three or four weeks, I suppose. Or if she's going to a show somewhere, she might come in to get a few bits and pieces of equipment, that sort of thing. We keep quite a lot of tack and stuff here, and of course we have all the grooming gear as well."

"Does her mother, Mrs Durnan, ever come with her?" Flynn asked.

"Nope. I've never seen anyone with her at all."

"OK. Thanks guys, that's very helpful. Oh, and if she does come in again soon, no need to mention we were asking questions," Flynn said.

The two men looked at each other and shrugged their shoulders in unison before returning to their work.

Chapter Nineteen

It was late afternoon by the time the team got back together for a briefing.

"OK, everyone, settle down. We have a lot to get through," Lyons said. She was allowing her frustration with being cooped up in the office, together with the lack of progress on the case, show rather more than it should.

"Now. Sally has had a really good result from the CCTV at the petrol station in Athlone. As you can see, we now have a mug shot of a person of interest connected to the grey van," Lyons said.

She went on to explain about the other material that had been found in the van, and informed the group that forensics were working on the evidence to try and get an identity for the driver.

"John, did you manage to scan the photo into the face matching software?"

"Yes, I did, boss. Nothing, I'm afraid."

"Is that because of the quality of the image, or is it because he's not in the database?" Flynn asked.

"No. The image is fine. I sharpened it up a good bit and it's pretty clear. Our man just isn't in there."

"Mmm. OK. Well, thanks for trying. Eamon, what have you got for us?"

Flynn recounted the visit to the Durnan's residence, and the little chat he had had with Ultan Whelan. Then he told them about Shauna Durnan's dealings with the Co-op in Athenry, leaving out the comments the men had made about her appearance.

"Right, so it looks as if there's a lot of cash swimming around. John, have you had a chance to look at Durnan's bank account yet?"

"I haven't done a full analysis, boss, but there is something odd OK."

"Go on."

"Well, the total throughput on his account over the last year is just €24,000. There are all the usual transactions that everyone pays by direct debit – you know: electric, property tax, phone bill, broadband, Netflix, that sort of thing – and a lot of card transactions for diesel. But the odd thing is that there's no evidence of anyone spending money on clothes, meals out, not even groceries. And the total just doesn't match up with the lifestyle. I'll have a better idea tomorrow when I've done a full trawl through," O'Connor said.

"Yes, but surely he could have had another bank account? Or maybe Mrs Durnan uses hers for all that other stuff," Flynn said.

"I've checked that. I can only find one bank account – it's a joint account with three debit cards issued on it," O'Connor said, a little defensively.

"OK, John. Good work. But have another good root around tomorrow. We need to be sure of our facts before we go accusing them of anything, but it does look as if Durnan was getting a pile of readies from somewhere, apart from the cash going through his bookie's business. Maybe Hamill was right after all. On the subject of which, there's an Inspector from SOCU coming down tomorrow to give us a hand," Lyons said, looking at Sally Fahy. Fahy's face reddened slightly.

"Don't worry, Sally, it's a female officer – Valerie White by name. She'll be here in the morning. Oh, before I forget, have we had any luck with the van that Deasy sold to this guy? Has it been spotted anywhere?"

The team looked from one to another, but no one spoke.

"I take it that's a no, then. Damn – it can't just have disappeared."

"Have you any idea how many small white vans there are in County Galway, boss? And he could easily have changed the plates by now as well," O'Connor said.

"I don't give a damn if he's hand-painted it in pink and yellow polka dots – we need to find it. Sally – can you ring around all the Garda stations in the area? Give them a shake-up. The damn thing can't have vanished into thin air. And has Sinéad got back to anyone with anything?"

Again, the team stayed silent, looking embarrassed.

"Right. I'll deal with that. Let's leave it for now, then. We'll meet again tomorrow, after I have welcomed Valerie Whiter than White – say, ten o'clock," Lyons said.

When Lyons got back to her desk, there was a message for her to call Mick Hays.

"Hi, Mick. You were looking for me," she said.

"Oh, hi, Maureen. Yes, I was. Listen, do you still need that presence outside Durnan's house? I'm getting fierce earache about the cost of it."

"Oh, shit. Sorry, Mick – but I could do with a couple more days if you can swing it. They've already picked up some really useful stuff for us. And there's definitely something iffy going on out there to do with ready cash."

"Hmm... OK. We'll do another 48 hours then. Don't suppose you could get one of your lot to do one of the shifts?"

"Not a chance, Mick. Sorry. They're all up to their eyes. But listen, let's keep going for another two days and then re-evaluate it. I won't keep the watch going any longer than absolutely necessary – promise. OK?"

"Yeah, OK. How's it all going anyway?"

Lyons gave Hays a brief account of developments to date, and told him about the imminent arrival of the replacement SOCU officer.

"Thanks. Sounds as if you're getting somewhere, at least. I'll see you later. Bye."

When she had finished the call, Lyons took stock of exactly where their case was going. She wasn't happy. The team were doing all that they could, but they needed something more – some kind of breakthrough that was so far eluding them. There wasn't quite enough 'probable cause' to get a warrant for Durnan's property, though she felt that, at some stage, they would have to search it thoroughly. There was undoubtedly a stash of hot money there somewhere, and they couldn't let that pass. Feeling very dejected, she decided to give Sinéad Loughran a call.

"Cheer me up, Sinéad. Tell me you have identified our mystery man and you have his address!" she said when she got through to the forensic lab.

"Nope – not a chance – sorry. We did get some DNA off the cigar stubs, and not a bad print from the back of the door handle from the van, but no matches anywhere. This guy is off the radar."

"Damn it, Sinéad, I was hoping you would have solved it for me by now. We're rightly stuck."

"Well, there is one tiny bit of good news."

"What's that?"

"Sand."

"Sand? Don't tease, Sinéad. What about sand?"

"We found some sand in the footwell on the driver's side of the VW van. And it's a very special kind of sand. Most sand is made by the grinding down of rocks over thousands of years."

"Yes, I know. I think I learnt that in first-year geography class, Sinéad," Lyons said.

"Ah, yes, but this sand is different. It's been made largely by the grinding down of sea shells, not stones. And there's only one place anywhere near here that has that type of sand," Loughran said.

"Where?"

"Dog's Bay, out the far side of Roundstone. You know – that beautifully curved, white sandy beach with the old abandoned caravan site."

"Yes, of course, I know it well – too well if truth be told. How much was there in the van?"

"Not a lot. I'd say it just came off the soles of the shoes of whoever was driving it."

"And you're sure about this, Sinéad?"

"Maureen Lyons – how can you even ask such a thing! Of course I'm sure. What time are you finishing up there?"

"In about half an hour – why?"

"Because you need alcohol, Maureen, by the sounds of things. And so do I. Meet in Doherty's in forty-five minutes?"

"Eh, yeah. OK. Just the one mind you, I need to get home," Lyons said.

"You're on."

When the call was ended, Lyons telephoned Pascal Brosnan at the Roundstone Garda station.

"Hi, Pascal. Listen, can you do something for me. Drive out to Tadgh Deasy's place and find out if he ever drove that VW van we lifted out to Dog's Bay. Make sure you get a straight answer from him, and let me know. Then, can you go down to Dog's Bay yourself and have a snoop around? See if there might be anyone camped out in the old caravan site, or anywhere round and about. If there is, don't disturb them. Just report back. OK?"

"Yes, fine, Inspector. I'll take Mary with me, and would it be OK to go in plain clothes? It might look less obvious."

"Yes, good idea. Thanks."

Chapter Twenty

The two women met in Doherty's pub, close to the Garda station, just before six o'clock. Loughran had got there first and had set up a nice cool glass of chardonnay for Lyons.

"God, I could kiss you, Sinéad – thanks."

"Steady on, Maureen. There's enough gossip around here without giving them more to natter about!"

"Oh, so what's the current set of rumours, then?" Lyons asked. She took a large mouthful of the wine. "Mmm, that's better."

"Ah, you know, just the usual crap. That business between Hamill and Sally Fahy has done the rounds, but it's more or less blown itself out by now. But there's a bit of a rumour going around about the SOCU thing."

"What SOCU thing?" Lyons said.

"You know. The fact that they're thinking about setting up a SOCU unit here in the West. And what with that officer coming down tomorrow, it's kind of fuelled the speculation."

"Jesus, Sinéad – that was only arranged a couple of hours ago. How did that get out so fast?"

"Well, you know what they say, 'if you want to get ahead – get ahead of the rumour mill'."

"You're obviously much better connected than I am in that department."

"I guess. See, people don't mind telling me all kinds of stuff, 'cos they think I'm not really a copper. You'd be amazed what I hear. Most of the guys are just trying to impress me with all their little nuggets of secret information to get into my knickers – but that's not happening," Loughran said.

Lyons laughed.

"On the subject of which, how is the love life?" she said.

"Don't even go there. Nada. Not a peep. I'm thinking of going on internet dating!"

"God, that bad, eh? But don't do that, Sinéad. It's full of weirdos, and if you get murdered, who would we have to chase down the clues?"

"Ha ha, very funny. I blame those white paper suits we have to wear at the scenes of crime. They really aren't very flattering."

"OK. I'll have to ask Mick to get Giorgio Armani to design the next lot we buy for you!"

Lyons stuck to her one drink before leaving Sinéad and going home. She always liked spending time with Loughran. They enjoyed the banter, and the somewhat irreverent chat about their often-grim work.

* * *

Lyons was at her desk the following morning just after nine o'clock when the desk sergeant called her to say that an Inspector Valerie White had arrived and was asking for her.

Lyons went downstairs to collect the woman and bring her back to her office.

White was five foot nine in height with shoulder-length blonde hair, striking bright blue eyes, and a fabulously slim figure.

Lyons thought to herself that she'd have to keep an eye on this one.

"Good morning, Inspector. I'm Senior Inspector Maureen Lyons. Welcome to Galway. Have a good drive down?" Lyons said.

"Yes, and I was most careful to keep well within the speed limit, especially passing Loughrea," Valerie White said.

"Oh that. Yes, I heard Inspector Hamill had a spot of bother," Lyons said.

"Serves him right – wanker," White said. She took a seat opposite Lyons' desk.

"Oh. He has a bit of a rep then?"

"We call him 'Feely Frank'. He's always trying to grope the female officers, and everyone knows that he does very little himself and just steps in at the end of an investigation to take the credit. But of course, no one says anything out loud. We still work in a very male-dominated world, Inspector Lyons."

Lyons was warming to the woman already.

"It's Maureen, Valerie. Just call me Maureen."

"OK. Thanks, and I'm Val, by the way."

The two inspectors spent the next hour discussing the situation regarding John Durnan and the suspicion that he may have been in some way involved with organised crime or drug gangs. Lyons raised the issue of the dodgy car dealer as well, and asked White if she thought there was any connection.

"That's where we'll start, if it's OK with you. I'd like to organise a raid on the garage run by Brendan Moran. We have enough evidence to show that he's at it, and if we turn over the place thoroughly, we could easily discover some very useful links. We'll need a few uniforms, and if we could get a dog handler too, it would make it look a lot better," White said.

"When do you want to do it?" Lyons asked.

"Tomorrow, early doors would be good. Can you organise a warrant?"

"Yeah, sure, that won't be a problem. And I'll arrange to get Joe Mason, our dog guy, out with his trusty hound too. What are your plans for the rest of the day?"

"I'd like to go over all the evidence you have written up on the Durnan case. Look over the interviews and so on. Would that be OK?"

"Yes, of course. And maybe you'd like to have dinner with my partner and I later on, unless you have other arrangements?" Lyons said.

"Oh, thanks. That would be lovely, and I promise not to try and snoop in your handbag! By the way, talking of gropers, is there any of your guys I should be wary of?"

Lyons laughed.

"No, you're OK there. My guys are house-trained. That's not to say they won't give you the once over – but they're strictly hands-free, my lot."

"That's a relief."

"But there is one thing you should know, Val. My partner is Superintendent Mick Hays – he's in overall charge of the detectives in this area. We live together."

"Wow. That's cool. Lucky you." Valerie White was a bit stuck for words.

"Wait till you meet him to make your mind up how lucky I am! No, but he's great, and we really get along. I know it's a bit odd, but it works well for us both. OK. So, I'll introduce you to John O'Connor and you can start reviewing the evidence. I'll catch up with you later," Lyons said.

She got up and led White out into the open plan and introduced her to the team.

When Lyons got back to her office, there was a message to call Pascal Brosnan, so she put a call through to the station in Roundstone.

"Hi, Pascal. It's Inspector Lyons."

"Hello, Inspector. Thanks for returning my call. I did those two little jobs yesterday evening. Firstly, Deasy said the only trip he made in the VW van was into Roundstone village to put some diesel in it. He didn't go anywhere near the beaches."

"And do you believe him, Pascal?"

"Yeah, I do. He's on his best behaviour for now 'cos he thinks we might be going to charge him with something."

"Good. By the way, we aren't going to charge him. It would never get past the DPP, but handy that we can keep him on his toes. Don't let on. What about Dog's Bay?"

"Oh yeah, Mary and I went down there in her car, in civvies. We went for a walk out along the headland and doubled back through the caravan site. There are a few old vans still left there in poor repair, but no sign of anyone. No recent rubbish left out anywhere, or anything like that. There is one old caravan that is in a bit better condition than the others, and there is a yellow gas bottle attached to it that is still about half full of gas. But no signs of life."

"Hmm, OK. Thanks Pascal, anything else?"

"No, that's it, Inspector."

"OK, thanks, Pascal. And say hello to Mary for me. Bye."

Chapter Twenty-One

Valerie White spent the day going over the evidence with John O'Connor and making arrangements for the raid on the garage the following morning. Lyons had secured the warrant that they would need, and had roped in a handful of uniformed officers to carry out the search of the premises, and provide support.

Lyons had been in touch with Joe Mason as well, and arranged for him to be at Moran's garage the following morning with Brutus, his German Shepherd dog. There wasn't really a need for Brutus – they wouldn't be doing any tracking, which was his speciality – but it always added weight to a situation when the dog and his handler came along. Even the most hardened criminals usually wilted when they saw the dog's fangs coming at them at full tilt.

The plan was to arrive at around half past nine and send the uniformed officers in along with Joe and the dog first. White would hang back in case there was any trouble with the owner, and then Lyons and herself would go in and carry out a thorough search of the premises, ably assisted by the uniformed squad.

By half past six in the evening all the arrangements were in place, and Lyons stopped in the open plan office to collect Valerie and take her out to dinner with Superintendent Hays.

"Ready for off, Val?" Lyons said.

"Yeah, ready when you are. I'll just get my jacket and my bag," she said.

She collected her stuff, and while she was slipping on her coat, Lyons asked, "So, Val. Are you hungry? What kind of grub do you fancy?"

"Yes, I sure am. I'm easy, but I hear the seafood is particularly good in these parts."

"You're right. I'll just give Mick a call and arrange to meet at the restaurant."

Lyons and White walked through to Shop Street and down all the way to the docks where one of their favourite seafood restaurants was located. O'Connaire's was always busy, but being regulars, Hays had managed to arrange a table for the three of them. As they walked along, Lyons asked White if she had found anything of interest in the Durnan file.

"Looks like there's something going on there, OK. We need a lot more evidence before we can tie it to organised crime, but I have a feeling there is a connection. What do you think, Maureen?"

"We have to be very careful with this one. We can't be seen to be harassing a bereaved family, but I agree, something isn't right. We need some kind of lucky break."

They reached the restaurant a few minutes later. When they were seated at the table on the first floor, looking out over the harbour, Lyons said, "So, who's the designated driver tonight then?"

"That would be me," Hays said, "you girls go on and have a couple of glasses of wine with your meal. I'll have a whiskey when we get home."

"Thanks, Superintendent. I'll be OK walking back in any case."

"Not at all. We'll drop you off later, and by the way, it's Mick when we're out socially."

As their meal progressed, Lyons decided to raise the somewhat sensitive subject of the SOCU plans for the region.

"Val, have you heard anything about the plans for a SOCU unit here in Galway?"

"Yes, of course. In fact, I've been on the panel for the last two years looking at the idea – how it would be funded; what level of manpower would be needed; what equipment; and so on. It's at quite an advanced stage."

"So, you think it's going to happen, then?" Lyons said.

"Well, you can never be certain till it's actually announced, but it looks like it. What have you heard, Mick?" White said.

"Not much, but that doesn't surprise me. When I heard you were coming down, I had a chat with Chief Superintendent Plunkett. He's of the same view that it will go ahead all right, probably just before the end of the year, or from January."

"Yes, I've met him once or twice at the meetings in Dublin. He seems like a wily enough old guy," White said.

Hays and Lyons were a bit surprised to hear their superior officer described in such terms, but they silently agreed that the description was not inaccurate.

"Finbarr is OK. You're right – he has a lot of political savvy, which I guess is why he's a Chief Super. But he gives us a lot of leeway. We have no complaints, do we Maureen?" Hays said.

"No, none at all, though to be honest, I don't have a lot to do with him. He's quite a man's man. I don't think he quite understands women in the force. He probably thinks we should be at home doing the vacuuming and washing the dishes. But he doesn't obstruct us, and he got me a bonus last year after a particularly nasty murder we had to deal with, so I can't complain."

"Yeah, and I got a new boat out of it, didn't I?" Hays said reaching out to squeeze Lyons' hand affectionately.

"What does your work involve anyway, Val?" Lyons asked.

"It's very varied. Much like your own, I guess. Lots and lots of desk work, research, that sort of thing. Then, ever so often, there is some mad action that could go one way or the other. We deal with some fairly nasty types from time to time. And of course, 'Mr Big' usually stays well out of it, so we're mostly dealing with the hired low-life," White said.

"Do you think being female makes any difference?" Lyons asked.

"Not really. Our team is pretty tight. We have to look out for each other, or someone could get badly hurt, or worse. Of course, there are always one or two pricks like Hamill hovering, but you learn how to deal with them after a while. Do you have any bother here – being female, I mean?"

"None. I don't think any of the guys would try to mess with me. Firstly, I can be a nasty cow when I choose, and of course I have excellent top cover." Lyons said looking warmly across at her partner. "I get on really well with Sally Fahy too – my sergeant. She's great."

As the meal came to an end, Lyons was amazed at how much food Val White had put away, and yet she was so slim. Lyons, too, had a very trim figure, but she had to work at it and was always careful about her calorie intake.

When they had finished eating and allowed a suitable interval to digest the scrumptious food, they left the restaurant and drove Valerie White back to her hotel.

* * *

On the way home in the car, Hays broached the subject of the imminent formation of a local SOCU in Galway with Lyons.

"Sounds as if this SOCU thing is game on. Would you fancy it?"

"Jesus, Mick. Are you serious? C'mon, truth now – what do you know that I don't know?"

"No, it's not like that, promise. But they'll be looking out for suitable officers to man the thing soon. And you're firearms trained and known as a very tough officer. I'd say you'd be an ideal candidate if you were interested. And don't forget, I'll almost certainly be asked for my input, if I'm not actually on the selection panel."

"That would be just fucking lovely. Me sitting there in front of you, with you cross questioning me about my suitability to go gang hunting, and me trying not to laugh."

"They might excuse me from that particular interview – but you never know. Would you be into it?"

"God, I don't know, Mick. I'd have to give it some serious thought. What would you think if I went for it?"

"I'd be shitting it every time you went out on a mission. But I wouldn't dream of obstructing you if you wanted it, and I'd support you all the way, you know that."

"You're a good man, Mick Hays," Lyons said. She moved closer to him and planted a kiss on his cheek as he drove along.

"Would I get any more money?"

"I think so. I'd have to look it up. I seem to remember there's a special allowance for Gardaí who want to get shot at, but I don't know how much it is. Not like you to be concerned with that, though. And I think they give you a souped-up BMW to drive too."

"That's it – count me in. No, I'm joking. But I'll give it some thought. Promise."

Chapter Twenty-Two

They all arrived at Moran's garage at almost the exact same time the following morning. The van carrying six Gardaí went in first, followed by Joe Mason and Brutus. The dog looked pretty intimidating barking its head off and snarling at anything that moved. Moran himself was in the portacabin with two other men, seated at a filthy table consuming tea and greasy breakfast rolls.

The sergeant that had the warrant with him showed it to Moran and instructed the three men to stay in the cabin while a search of the premises was taking place. After a few minutes, they realised that Moran wasn't likely to try and shoot them or get violent in any way, and the sergeant signalled White and Lyons to come on into the yard.

Valerie White concentrated on what was laughingly referred to as the office. It was no such thing. Just bundles of paper piled on top of an old wooden dresser, and a box that seemed to contain registration documents and UK MOT certificates. Another grimy wooden box about the size of a shoe box had several sets of keys in it.

As White started to go through the paperwork, one of the uniformed Gardaí came into the cabin.

"Mam, we've found a load of English number plates stashed in the shed down behind the bench. And there's a BMW jeep that's being parted out there too. Jack is just checking it now to see if it's been stolen. It's come from Northern Ireland."

"Good work. Keep looking, and make it thorough," White said, and then, addressing Brendan Moran, "what have you got to say for yourself then, Mr Moran?"

Moran said nothing, but kept staring down at his dirty mug half filled with strong tea. The other two men shuffled nervously in their seats.

The search continued, and it revealed that several vehicles in the yard that appeared to have Irish registrations, were in fact British. The number plates that they wore were fictional, and when White matched them up with logbooks from the office, it became clear that the paperwork was forged. With a little more searching she found a wad of around thirty blank Irish registration documents stuffed into a drawer. White called two of the uniformed officers inside.

"Stay here with these three, will you, Guard, and if anyone gives you any trouble, introduce them to Joe's dog. I don't think he's had any breakfast yet, so he's likely hungry!"

White left the scruffy office and found Lyons wandering around outside.

"Well – what did you find?" Lyons asked.

"Plenty. Enough to charge the lot of them in any case. We'll take them to three separate Garda stations for questioning."

"Will they give you any information about who's behind this lot?"

"Not a chance. They wouldn't last a week if they did. But that's not how we operate, Maureen. We just keep hassling these guys. Keep taking their stuff, and their money, and eventually they'll get fed up and go somewhere else where it's easier to make a few dishonest quid. And some day, if we get lucky, we'll turn over a big stone and underneath it will be one of the gang leaders. But we won't find him here."

"Did you get anything on the grey VW van?" Lyons asked.

"The paperwork will be in there somewhere. We'll bring all that stuff back to Dublin where my team will have plenty of time to sort through it. But before we go, I need to see if we can get our hands on the money."

"Won't that be in the bank?"

"Not likely. These sorts don't trust banks!" Valerie White said.

"Brutus might be able to help with that. He's trained to search for cash. Hang on, I'll get Joe over."

Lyons called Joe Mason over and explained that Inspector White believed that there could be money stashed around the yard somewhere.

"These kinds of people don't usually bank their money. Do you think Brutus might be able to locate it?"

"Maybe. But it's pretty dangerous around here. There's a lot of sharp edges and broken glass. I don't want him to get hurt," Mason said.

"No, of course not. Have you got any of those cute little leather bootees for him?"

"Good thinking. Yes, I have them in the van. I'll go and sort it out."

Lyons watched as the remaining Gardaí continued to root around in the dirty old galvanised shed where the BMW was being dismantled. They found an old brown envelope that had fifty or sixty UK tax discs in it, and gave it to Inspector White as well.

A few minutes later, Joe Mason called out.

"Inspector Lyons – over here."

Mason was standing at the back of an old rusty black Audi with the boot open. When Lyons clambered over the rubbish and got to it, Mason pointed to the boot floor where a compartment had been welded in. Brutus was standing beside his handler looking very pleased with himself, and Lyons patted his head saying, "Good boy, Brutus. Who's a clever dog then?"

Brutus licked her hand.

The hideaway held a metal box with a stout padlock on it. Mason put on vinyl gloves and lifted it clear, handing it to Lyons.

Back on safer ground, Lyons gave the box over to Valerie White.

"I think this may be what you were looking for, Val. It feels pretty heavy. I'd say there's a good few quid in there."

"Fantastic. Thanks, Maureen; and thank Mason too. It was lucky you brought him out. We'd never have found that without the dog."

"All part of the service. What happens now? Have you got what you came for?" Lyons asked.

"These idiots are only the foot soldiers – the very dispensable flotsam and jetsam that the gangs use to do their dirty work. So, now we spend weeks pouring through all this stuff, seeing if we can find any connection to the organisers of this lot. Maybe, just maybe, we'll find that one of the big guys is riding around in one of these cars – but we'll need to get lucky. I'd like to get going, if that's OK with you? We'll get these three stooges off to a nice cold custody cell somewhere, while we go through all the stuff we found. Then we'll charge them with receiving; forging documents; theft; and the money will get handed over to the Criminal Assets Bureau. There might be enough to pay for a football pitch for a school somewhere. Listen, thanks for your hospitality last night. It was good to meet Mick and learn a bit about your set-up. I was thinking – I'm going to stay over one more night. Would you be up for a meet later on? There's something I'd like to talk to you about. Just us two," White said.

"Yeah, sure. Give me a call when you get sorted and we'll fix something up."

"Great. Thanks. See ya."

* * *

When Lyons got back to her office, Eamon Flynn followed her in.

"Hi, boss. Have you got a minute?"

"Sure, Eamon. Give me a moment to get my jacket off, and I'm dying for a cup of tea."

"You might want to leave it on, boss. I've had a call from Ultan Whelan. He's one of the Gardaí that's been on sentry duty out at the Durnans'. He's busting to talk to us, but I said I'd wait till you got back and then maybe we'd drive out to see him," Flynn said.

"Hmm, OK. Give him a call back, but I don't want to meet him outside the house. Arrange some convenient watering hole this side of Ballinasloe and we'll go and meet him. But I must have a cuppa first, so tell him not to hurry."

"Right, boss. How did you get on out beyond?"

"Pretty good. Loads of stuff for Inspector White, but I'll tell you more on the drive out. I have to have a cup of tea – now!"

Flynn called Whelan back and arranged to meet him at a roadhouse close to Ballinasloe called Conway's. The place stayed open all day, and served food and drink until late. Rural pubs in Ireland had gone into steep decline since the new, more rigorous, drink-driving laws had been introduced and were now being enforced, so they had to do whatever they could to keep turnover going. Lyons asked John O'Connor to get her a much-needed cup of tea, and she drank it quickly so as not to hold up the meeting.

On the way out in Lyons' car, she brought Eamon Flynn up to speed on the goings-on at Moran's garage.

"Nice one. Gives the SOCU something to take back to Dublin, anyway. Will we get anything out of it?" Flynn asked.

"Maybe just a bit more information about the VW van. But I doubt if our man was involved. I'd say he just bought it at Moran's 'cos it was cheap."

Chapter Twenty-Three

When Lyons and Flynn arrived at Conway's, they saw Whelan's Garda car parked outside.

"He's keen," Lyons said.

"Yeah, well, I think he might have been up all night."

"Oh, OK. We'll let him tell the story."

They found Ultan Whelan easily enough inside, as the place was quite empty at that time of day. Flynn introduced Lyons, and the three of them sat in a quiet spot well away from the few other patrons.

"So, Ultan, what's the story?" Lyons said.

"I was on duty last night outside Durnan's house. I swapped with another lad because he wanted the night off, so I was doing the graveyard shift from twelve to eight. I was dozing off in the car at about two-ish, when lights coming down the drive woke me. It was Shauna in the family jeep."

"Interesting. What did you do?" Flynn said.

"Well, I know it's not exactly following instructions, but I tailed her. It was nice and dark, and I kept my own lights off, so she didn't see me," Whelan said.

"Where did she go?" Lyons said.

"That's the weird part. She drove on to Galway, and then out along the N59, turning left after Recess and going through Roundstone. Then she turned onto a little track down towards the sea. I parked up at the top of the lane and followed her down on foot, staying in the shadows. At the bottom of the lane, there was a small white van parked. She got in, and a few minutes later, she and a bloke got out and went into the caravan site. I couldn't get too close, but they went into one of the old vans, and by the sounds of things, and the movement of the van, they weren't just talking."

"Jesus. Were they having sex?" Lyons asked.

"I'd say so, but I can't be sure. I didn't want to get caught. She stayed about forty-five minutes and then she left on her own," Ultan Whelan said.

"Did you get the number of the van?" Flynn said.

"Yes, of course. And I checked it in the system. It's registered to a company in Loughrea, but they say they handed it back a few weeks ago when the lease was up. I'd say the change of ownership just hasn't been logged yet."

"Did you follow her back? Did she stop anywhere else?" Lyons asked.

"No. She went straight back home. We got there just as the sun was coming up. I've been trying to contact you to tell you all day, Inspector."

"That's OK, Ultan, don't worry about it. We know now. So, Shauna has a boyfriend after all. Interesting.

Look, you need to get some rest. Is there some cover for tonight at the house?"

"Yeah, it's fine. Derry will be on tonight," Whelan said.

"Right. Well, tell Derry if Shauna sets off again tonight, just call it in. Tell him not to follow her, OK?"

"Right, no bother," Whelan said.

* * *

Flynn and Lyons left Conway's and set off back to Galway.

On the way back, Lyons asked Flynn what he made of Ultan Whelan's report.

"Well, the girl lied to us for starters. She told you she didn't have a boyfriend, and that's clearly not the case. But I'm not sure it's that significant – she may not have wanted her folks to know about it," Flynn said.

"Yes, but what about that business with the white van? That's a coincidence, and as you know I don't like coincidences. Why don't you give Tadgh Deasy a call and verify the reg number with him? See if that's the same white van he sold to the guy who traded in the Volkswagen."

Flynn made the call as Lyons drove along.

"Nope. The numbers don't tally, but that doesn't entirely surprise me. Our client seems to have access to lots of dodgy stuff. What's your plan now, boss?"

"I'm thinking, Eamon. I'll let you know when I have one," Lyons said. They covered the remaining few kilometres into Galway in silence.

* * *

"Sally, could you pop in to my office for a few minutes please?" Lyons said when they had returned to the station.

When the two were seated in her office, Lyons revealed her plan.

"I need a favour, Sally. Can you hook up with Pascal Brosnan out in Roundstone and set up a lookout on the old caravan site at Dog's Bay with him tonight? I'd ask Eamon, only he's busy, and I have to meet Valerie White for dinner – she wants to do a girls' night out. I think she has something on her mind that she wants to talk about one to one."

"Yes, sure. What are we looking for?"

Lyons told Fahy about Ultan Whelan's adventures in the early hours of the previous morning.

"I think whoever Shauna was visiting last night out there could be a person of interest to us. I don't have anything concrete to go on, but there's something not right about it, and it's niggling me. If a guy in a white van turns up, lift him back to the station in Roundstone and give him a good grilling. Then call me, OK?"

"OK. Do you want to tell me anything more?" Fahy asked.

"There's not a lot more to tell. There may be nothing in it, but I just have a feeling about this. Humour me, will you?"

"Yeah, no problem. Your hunches have proven dead on before, so who am I to argue?"

"Thanks, Sally. And a night at the beach with the lovely Pascal Brosnan can't be all bad, can it?"

"Behave, boss. I'm more interested in the overtime, to be truthful."

"Whatever," Lyons said. But she wasn't convinced.

* * *

Lyons collected Valerie White from the Imperial Hotel at seven o'clock as arranged.

"Hi, Maureen. Thanks for collecting me. I hope you don't mind, but I've booked The Old Cottage out in Moycullen for us. I hear it's very good," White said when they were seated in Lyons' Volvo.

"Oh, nice. I haven't been there in a while. Mick took us there for our so-called anniversary two years ago. It was really very good," Lyons said.

"How long have you two been together?"

"God, it must be five years now. It started when we were out in Poland working on a murder case together. He was just an inspector then, and I was a sergeant. I know it's a bit unconventional, but it works for us. We have a rule never to take the job inside the house."

"He's a very good-looking man, and he seems really nice with it," White said.

"He is. Have you anyone special?"

"Hmm… kind of, but it's complicated. I'll tell you another time."

Lyons decided not to probe her companion any further on the matter. Perhaps when she had a few glasses of wine inside her, she would be more forthcoming.

* * *

The two women were shown to a secluded table at the restaurant, but they still managed to turn a few heads as they took their seats. Valerie White was looking stunning, and Lyons was equally impressive in a light summer dress with her shoulder-length dark hair shining in the subtle lighting.

They ordered their meals from the extensive à la carte menu, and Lyons insisted that White should have a glass of wine, while she stayed on the Perrier water as she was driving.

"I'm sorry, Val, but I have to leave my phone on. We have an operation on out west tonight, and I have to be on stand-by."

"Story of my life. Don't worry about it. I understand."

When the starters had been served, and the two detectives had polished them off leaving not a morsel on their plates, Valerie White raised the reason for their meeting.

"Have you thought any more about the SOCU thing, Maureen?"

"Not a lot, to be honest. I haven't had the time, what with this Durnan thing. Why do you ask?"

"Well, I'm sorry, Maureen, but I haven't been entirely honest with you and Superintendent Hays."

"Go on," Lyons said uneasily.

"There's a bit of an ulterior motive for my being here. Sure, we had to deal with Moran, but as I was coming down here anyway, I was asked to do a bit of scouting for the new unit," White said.

"I see. So, it's definitely going ahead, then?"

"Oh, yes. There's no doubt. And we need some top-class officers to get involved. It will be a big deal for the brass. The first SOCU outside Dublin. There will be a lot of media attention on it too, so results will be vital, and you have an excellent track record in that department."

"Is this an interview?" Lyons said. She was a bit prickly.

"No, no. That all comes later. But they don't want to make a full-frontal approach without sounding you out first," White said, and then she had the good sense to stay quiet.

Their main courses arrived. White was having duck with a cherry and spice sauce with dauphinoise potatoes, while Lyons had opted for pan-fried venison. Both plates of food looked sumptuous, and they were served their vegetables by a waiter in an immaculate black suit and white shirt with a bow tie.

When Lyons had eaten half of her meal, she said to White, "So, what conclusion have you come to, if any?"

"There's little doubt you would be a definite asset to the unit. I like the way Eamon Flynn operates too, but I'm not sure if Superintendent Hays would appreciate the detectives being left with no one senior."

"You're right about that. He's said he wouldn't stand in my way if I want to go for it, but taking Flynn out as well might be a step too far. If you're looking for another good candidate, there's a lassie out in Roundstone that shows a lot of promise. She's still quite new, but she'll make a fine officer in time. And Séan Mulholland in Clifden has a young guy that is top notch. Peadar Tobin by name. I've worked with him a bit and he's very reliable."

"Well, if you go for it, it would be up to you to staff the unit, subject to some basic ground rules, of course."

"So, you'd see me as the senior officer, then?"

"Oh, yes, of course," White said.

"Val, I don't know how much you know about my record in the force, but I have some pretty unusual techniques. I don't often play by the book."

"You mean tripping up and arresting a bank robber single handedly when you were a rookie; shooting at a villain that had just shot your partner; getting thrown into a deep bog hole after you'd been kidnapped and managing to escape – that sort of thing?"

"You have been doing your homework, haven't you?" Lyons said.

White just smiled back.

"Sounds like perfect qualifications for SOCU, if you ask me. We're not looking for shrinking violets, Maureen."

Lyons' phone rang.

She answered it, looking more and more serious as the call progressed. When she finished, she said to White, "Sorry, I have to go. Come with me if you want to see up close and personal how we do things out here."

Chapter Twenty-Four

The phone call was from Pascal Brosnan. He was distraught.

"Inspector, Inspector, Sergeant Fahy has been hurt. She's bad. She's out cold, and her head is bleeding. I've called the ambulance but it will take them ages to get here. What should I do?"

"Calm down, Pascal. Firstly, where are you?" Lyons said as gently as she could manage.

"On the lane down to Dog's Bay, in an entrance behind a wall. This is all my fault."

"OK. Now listen, Pascal, you have to stay calm. Is Sally breathing?"

There was a pause in the conversation while Brosnan went to check on Fahy.

"Yes. She is, Inspector."

"Right, well now, remember your first aid. Get her onto her side and make sure she can't swallow her tongue, and then get her warm. Don't have her lying on the cold ground – put your coat underneath her and something over her. Are there any other injuries you can see?"

There was a minute's silence whilst Brosnan attended to the limp form of Sally Fahy lying on the ground.

"I'm back," Brosnan said, "and no, I can't see any other injuries."

"OK. Is her head wound still bleeding?"

"Not really – just kinda oozing a bit."

"Right, well put something over it and apply just a little pressure – see if you can stop it. But don't press too hard, you could make matters worse."

"OK, Inspector. Give me a minute."

Brosnan was back on the line a few moments later.

"I'm on my way out there now. Any sign of the ambulance yet?" Lyons said.

"No, not yet. God, I hope she'll be all right. It looks bad."

"Just stay with her, Pascal, and make sure she doesn't get too cold. Don't move her more than you have to. Wait till the paramedics get there. Is she still unconscious?"

"Yes, she is. And she's real pale."

"That's to be expected. Does the ambulance know exactly where to go to?"

"Yes. I gave them the location and the driver knows it, or so he said."

"OK. How's her breathing now?"

"A bit better. Not as shallow as it was, and her skin is a bit warmer to the touch."

"Good. Hold her hand gently and let me know if she squeezes it or if there is any movement at all. I'll stay on the line. I have Inspector White with me too. We'll be there shortly."

Lyons pushed the Volvo as hard as she dared along the bumpy road between Oughterard and Maam Cross, and then on the N341 that would take them into Roundstone. She asked Valerie White to call Eamon Flynn and let him know what had happened.

"Get him to go into the station, and ask him to call Séan Mulholland at home as well and put him in the picture. I want him on stand-by. I've a feeling we're not finished with this for the night yet."

* * *

Garda Derry Devlin was settling down for what he thought would be a handy bit of overtime keeping watch on the Durnans' house at Nutfield Cross. He had provisioned himself well with a couple of good thick sandwiches, two bars of chocolate, and a flask of strong coffee for the night shift that lay ahead. He had even managed to rig up a few films on his iPad, so that he wouldn't be bored out of his mind sitting in the car for eight hours.

"Bit of a daft caper, this," he mused to himself as the night set in. It was a damp and cloudy night so there was no light of any kind anywhere around him, save for the distant glow from the Durnans' house at the other end of the long drive.

Devlin was just settling in to the first of his downloaded movies having devoured the sandwiches, washed down with two large cups of coffee, when he was disturbed by the arrival, at some speed, of a white Ford van that came up the road and skidded to a halt in the Durnans' entrance. A young man got out and punched a number onto the keypad, and the black wrought iron gates began to swing slowly inwards.

The young man jumped back into the van and sped off up the drive, the vehicle throwing up dust and stones as the wheels struggled for grip on the loose gravel.

Devlin was out of his car pretty quickly, and just managed to get through the gates as they closed over again. This was the van that everyone had been told to look out for, and here it was, right in front of him.

Devlin sprinted up along the drive, wishing he hadn't eaten so much of his meal in such a hurry. When he got close to the house, he kept well over to the side, hoping that he wouldn't be spotted. By this time, the white van was parked untidily in front of the house, and was unoccupied. Devlin crept around behind it and edged his way to the driver's door. The window had been left open enough for him to put his arm in and remove the keys from the ignition without having to open the door, which would have turned on the interior light and perhaps given his presence away. He then retreated to the cover of the beech hedge at the edge of the driveway, and called Mill Street.

When Flynn took the call, he gave instructions to the young Garda.

"Right. Stay where you are. Don't attempt an intervention till we get there. I'll come over immediately, and we'll get some of the locals out to you as well. They should be there in ten minutes or so. But stay out of sight. No heroics. This chap could be dangerous."

But seconds after Devlin had called the situation in, the door of the house opened, and Shauna Durnan and the lad from the van came out carrying two large sports bags. Mrs

Durnan was behind them, and Shauna turned and gave her a hug before getting into the black 4x4 that she normally drove, and opening the passenger's door for her companion.

The two set off at a brisk pace down the drive and out the gates. There was nothing Devlin could do, except wait for them to depart, and then call Inspector Flynn again. He was too far away from his own vehicle to give chase, and in any case, he had been warned not to leave his post at the house in no uncertain terms.

"Inspector Flynn, it's Derry Devlin here again. He's taking off with the young one from the Durnans' in her jeep. They were away down the drive and off down the road before I could get back to my car. I'm sorry, sir."

"Jesus, Derry. Which way did they go?" Flynn said, stepping on the accelerator in his own car.

"They turned right out the drive, so away from Ballinasloe anyway."

"Christ, there's a whole rabbit warren of roads and lanes up that way. They could be headed anywhere, and we'll never manage to put roadblocks on all those little boreens. Did you get the number of the jeep?"

"Yes. It's a black Land Cruiser 172G76990, and it's covered in mud and God knows what else, if that helps," Devlin said.

"Right. Stay where you are. I'll be there in ten minutes. Any sign of any of the local boys showing up yet?" Flynn said.

"No, sir, not yet."

* * *

Brosnan stepped out into the narrow track that led down to Dog's Bay as the ambulance lurched its way slowly in his direction. When it pulled up, two paramedics in green jumpsuits alighted, and Pascal showed them where Sally Fahy was, still lying unconscious on the ground behind the wall.

The paramedics got to work on her quickly. Jane put a canula into the back of her left hand and injected a clear liquid in through the arrangement.

"What's that you're giving her?" Brosnan asked.

"Adrenalin. We need to get her awake and bring her heart rate up if we can, so we can assess her condition."

When she had finished with the injection, she put in another line connected to a clear plastic bag marked 'Saline'. After a few moments, the Adrenalin started to take effect, and with the male paramedic gently slapping Sally's free hand, he said, "Sally, Sally, wake up, love, you're all right, we're here now. Wake up, girl."

Brosnan thought the man was being a bit severe on her, but after a few more goes, Fahy began to stir and moan, and seconds later she opened her eyes.

"Where am I?" she managed, much to everyone's relief.

"You're OK now, love. Just tell me, where does it hurt?" the man said.

"My head, oh Jesus, my head is bursting."

"We'll give you something for that in a minute. Can you move your legs?"

Fahy moved both her legs quite freely and confirmed to the paramedic that the rest of her seemed to be OK.

"Great. In a minute, we'll see if you can stand up – with our help of course. But there's no rush. Jane, give Sally something for her headache, will you?"

Jane inserted another phial of chemicals in through the canula.

"Did you get him, Pascal? Little bastard!" Fahy said, now recovering some of her fighting spirit.

"No, sorry, Sarge. He got away. I'm really sorry. I shouldn't have left you."

The paramedics were lifting Fahy up gently, gripping her under her arms, when Lyons' car pulled in behind the ambulance.

"God, Sally, are you OK?" Lyons said, walking over to where the paramedics were supporting Fahy between them. She was still very unsteady, and looked frighteningly pale.

The male paramedic answered for her.

"She's had a nasty bang on the head. We need to get her into hospital now."

"Right, yes, of course. Don't let me delay you."

"If you could just move your car, please," Jane said to Lyons.

"I'll go with her in the ambulance," Brosnan said.

"No, Pascal. She's in good hands now. You come with me. We need to talk. We'll go back to the station in Roundstone. I'll be along to see you later, Sally."

"Thanks, boss, but there's no need, I'll be fine."

"Go on – get yourself patched up. See you later."

Chapter Twenty-Five

Flynn had been busy on his car phone as he drove the last part of the journey to meet Derry Devlin at Nutfield Cross. He had set the wheels in motion for roadblocks on all the main roads leading away from Ballinasloe, but it was hard to muster a lot of resources at that time of night, so he had little confidence that the two would be caught.

Flynn barked out some orders to the uniformed Gardaí who had arrived out from the local station, and then turned to Devlin.

"C'mon, Derry, you're with me. We're going to have a little chat with the lady of the house!"

They drove up along the driveway again, having called ahead to get the gates opened. Jessica Durnan wasn't exactly pleased to see them, but she invited them in all the same, and brought them to the kitchen where they were offered tea.

"Mrs Durnan, we need to know who that man that arrived here in the white Ford van outside is please," Flynn said, getting straight to the point.

"Him. Oh, he's a nobody. He lends a hand now and then around the place, you know, with the horses and that sort of thing," she said dismissively.

"And his name?"

"Fintan something or other. He's a townie," Mrs Durnan said, as if she was describing the lowest form of life.

"Where is he now?" Flynn said.

"How should I know? I'm not his mother."

"Mrs Durnan, I have ten officers searching the stables and the grounds here right now as we speak. It would be a lot better for you if you just told us what you know. And while we're at it, where's Shauna?"

"You can't do that! Have you got a warrant? Don't you know I've just recently lost my husband, and here you are, harassing me as if I was some kind of criminal myself."

"We don't need a warrant, Mrs Durnan. We are carrying out a legitimate search for a fugitive we believe may have seriously wounded one of my officers earlier this evening. So, your co-operation would be much appreciated."

Flynn had decided that it would be best not to go in heavy handed when dealing with the woman. He favoured a gentler approach, but if that didn't work, he was quite prepared to get a lot tougher.

"Now, I'll ask again, where's Shauna?"

"Your guess is as good as mine. She took off with that good for nothing a while ago, and before you ask, I have no idea where they were heading. But you already know this. He was snooping around here when they left," she said pointing to Derry Devlin.

Before Flynn could respond, a uniformed Garda appeared at the back window and beckoned him to come out.

Flynn excused himself and went to join the man outside.

"Sir, you need to see this," he said, gesturing towards the stables.

The two men walked together to the stable block, and the uniformed man led the way into one of the stalls. The straw had been swept back revealing a sort of trap door in the floor, and several fifty euro notes were scattered around on the ground.

"Looks like someone left in a hurry," Flynn said. "OK. Bag up this lot and have another look around. See if there's anything else we need to secure. I'll be back in the house."

Once indoors again, Flynn changed his tactics.

"Right, Mrs Durnan. I'd like you to give me your mobile phone, please – now! As I'm sure you are aware, we have found your little hidey-hole out the back where you kept all the cash, and I'm not happy about the way Shauna left with this Fintan bloke. I'm going to place a female officer here overnight, and then I want you to come into the Garda station in Galway tomorrow morning to help us with our enquiries. You may want to have a solicitor present."

Jessica Durnan turned to face Flynn with a look of hatred in her eyes.

"What exactly is it that you think I have done, Inspector Flynn?" she said.

"I'm not sure yet, Mrs Durnan, but I intend to find out just what's been going on here. There's something not right. So, Garda Devlin here will arrange the officer to stay with you till the morning."

Flynn nodded to Derry Devlin and then got up and left the house.

Outside, he scrolled down through the contact list on Jessica Durnan's phone. He made a note of Shauna's number, and saw that there was an entry for a Fintan Casey, which he assumed was the 'nobody' the woman had referred to.

He called John O'Connor.

When he had apologised to O'Connor for disturbing him at the late hour, he gave him the two numbers and asked O'Connor if he could set up a trace on them both and see if they could be located.

* * *

Lyons, White and Brosnan arrived back at the Garda station at the edge of Roundstone when they had seen Sally Fahy off in the ambulance. Given that she was considered to be walking wounded, the paramedics had decided to take her all the way into Galway, rather than have her treated at the small hospital in Clifden.

Brosnan opened up the station, which had been in darkness, and when they were all inside, he said, "Shall I put the kettle on?"

"Yes, please, Pascal, I could do with a cuppa," Lyons said.

When the tea had been handed out, Lyons got down to business.

"OK, Pascal, so tell us what happened."

"I'm really sorry, Inspector. It was all my fault. We were set up for a kind of stakeout, watching out for that white van that everyone's been on about. We hid Sergeant Fahy's car behind the wall, but we had clear sight down the lane and would have been able to see any comings and goings. But my phone was back up at the house, so I left Sally in the car for a few minutes while I went back up to get it. I was only gone about ten minutes – fifteen at the most. When I got back, Sally was out of the car, lying on the ground. She'd obviously been attacked. God, I'm so sorry."

"Did you see anyone around when you got back from getting your phone?" Lyons asked.

"No. But as I was walking back, I did hear the sound of a car's engine taking off. But I was up around the bend in the road at that stage, so I didn't see anything. I didn't think there was anything in it, till I found Sally – sorry – Sergeant Fahy. I hope she'll be OK."

"I think she'll be fine, Pascal. Us Galway girls have very hard heads. But you definitely shouldn't have left her alone like that."

"God, I know. Will there be a disciplinary?"

"Let me talk to Sergeant Fahy when she's feeling a bit better. I'm going to leave you to tell Sergeant Mulholland tomorrow morning. OK?" Lyons said.

"Yes, yes of course."

Lyons and White left Pascal Brosnan in Roundstone feeling very sorry for himself, and drove back to the city.

On the way back to Galway, Lyons got a call from Eamon Flynn who brought her up to date on the developments at the Durnan house. When she had finished the call, she said to Valerie White, "I'll drop you off at your hotel, Val. It looks as if it's going to be a long night."

"Thanks. I don't think I'm adding much to the proceedings in any case. But if you don't mind me saying, I think you handled that situation very well. I probably would have torn the head off Brosnan, but it would have been the wrong thing to do."

"Not my style, Val. Oh, sure, I can be as tough as you like when the occasion calls for it. But Pascal is a good cop. He was clearly very upset about what happened. He'll be hard enough on himself over it without me piling in too," Lyons said.

"I can see that you're all very tight and supportive out here. It's almost a shame to break the spell."

"How do you mean?"

"Well, you know, with you possibly leaving the detective unit to go to SOCU, and all that."

"Ah, they'll get over it. They're a good bunch."

"So, you think you'll go for it, then?"

"I'm still thinking about it. We'll see."

Chapter Twenty-Six

Lyons left Valerie White at her hotel and continued on to the Garda station at Mill Street.

When she got in, Flynn and O'Connor were already there.

"Any news on the phones, John?"

"Yes, boss. We have a ping from Shauna's phone. It's a mast out near Mountbellew. Nothing from the other one."

"Is she still on the move?"

"No. It's been connected to that mast for a while now."

"OK, thanks. Eamon, can you call Jessica Durnan? Find out where her closest relatives live. Don't make any mention of Mountbellew. Just ask her."

Although it was very late, Lyons called Mick Hays to tell him all that had happened since she went out for a meal with Valerie White.

"I was wondering where you'd got to. That's dreadful. Will Sally be OK?"

"Yes, I think so, but she got a nasty bang on the head. But she's made of tough stuff – she'll be fine in a few days. Look, I'm going to be on this for most of the night. We think the suspect is holed up somewhere out near Mountbellew. We're going to have to launch a dawn raid if we can get the address. You OK?"

"Yeah, of course. Do you need anything from me?" Hays said.

"No, I think we're OK. I may have to get the Armed Response Unit out – we're not sure what we're dealing with here."

"Well, you be careful now, do you hear? We don't want any more casualties."

"It's OK. I won't go myself, this time. I'll stay here and co-ordinate things. I'll get Eamon to go out with them if it comes to it. Look, I'd better get on – there's a lot to organise."

"OK. Talk later. Bye."

When Lyons was off the call, Flynn came into her office.

"Jessica Durnan has a sister over near Mountbellew. It's a farm – quite a big one too. My guess is they are either hiding out there without the sister knowing, or she's taken them in. I've been onto the local boys, and they're calling me back with details."

Lyons went to the wall where she had a large map of the area pinned up.

"Hmm... well, get onto Moylough and Ballygar too. Get a good number of men lined up and I'll alert the ARU. Are you OK to go in with them at around 5 a.m.?"

"Yeah, sure. But do you not think that's a bit heavy handed, boss? After all, what have they really done? It's not as if they're exactly Bonny and Clyde," Flynn said.

"Ask Sally Fahy what they've done – well, this Fintan fella anyway. No, Eamon, we need to bring them in. This whole thing smells all wrong. It has done from the start. I mean, who robs a bookie of twenty grand and then chucks the money in a ditch? And that Jessica Durnan is hiding something, too. No, let's go and get them, and we'll be able to sort it out. If nothing else, the ARU will scare the bejaysus out of them. And unless I'm mistaken, whatever they have been up to, they're rank amateurs. Let's go with plan A."

When Flynn got back to his desk, he noticed that there was a text message on Jessica Durnan's phone, which he had confiscated earlier.

> *Hi mum. At Aunt Maeve's. All good. Don't worry. I'll call you tomoz. X*

"Gotcha! Nice one, Shauna. Thank you."

* * *

The teams were all assembled along the side of the R358 on the Caltra Road by half past four in the morning. Flynn had managed to assemble ten men from the surrounding stations, as well as from Tuam, which was not that far away. The ARU had turned out too, and there were four of them – three men and a woman officer, all highly trained and looking menacing in their black jumpsuits and baseball hats. They had six vehicles between them.

Flynn called the senior ARU officer over and a uniformed sergeant that was in charge of the other Gardaí.

"Right. You know the drill. We go in loud and fast. Blues and sirens. Two cars go round the back to cut off any possible escape, and the rest take on the front. Two knocks, wait ten seconds, and then use the big red key – OK? We're looking for a young lad called Fintan and a girl of about twenty called Shauna. Ignore everyone else, unless they have a weapon."

Their plan went like clockwork.

They knocked heavily on the front door as soon as officers were in position at the rear of the house. They waited the ten seconds as arranged, and then smashed the door open with a battering ram. The Armed Response Unit's men went in first, and as they entered the building, they shouted out loudly, "Armed Police! Stay where you are. Armed Police!"

It was all over in under two minutes. Fintan and Shauna were found together in a double bed in one of the upstairs bedrooms. The Gardaí handcuffed them both, and then separated them, putting them in the back of two different Garda cars, so that they had no chance to synchronize their stories.

Shauna's aunt, Maeve, was completely horrified at what was taking place. But the fright that she got seeing armed Garda officers coming at her up the stairs had rendered her silent, and she didn't regain the power of speech till it was all over.

The instruction from Lyons was to bring the two prisoners back to Galway and put them in two separate cells, making sure that they had no means of communicating with one another at any stage before they were questioned.

Lyons waited till they arrived back, and asked Flynn how it had all gone.

"Piece of cake, boss. No trouble, but I'm glad we had the troops out. It makes the whole thing a lot easier."

"Any weapons discharged?" she said.

"Not a bit of it. They came quietly. I think they were half asleep till we got them back here, to be honest."

"Right, well, tomorrow morning, you take Fintan and I'll interview Shauna. Let's see what all this is about. I'm going over to the hospital to see how Sally is. I'll catch you later. Say, ten o'clock?"

"Righto, boss. Give Sally my best wishes if she's awake."

"Will do. Good night, or should I say good morning."

* * *

Sally was in a private room beside St Agatha's ward in the hospital. She was dozing when Lyons arrived, but the general melee of the place, and the early start that saw things coming to life well before six in the morning, prevented her from getting any decent sleep.

Fahy was connected up to a fairly serious looking monitoring machine that was beeping away quietly beside her. She had a bag of something slowly being released into her hand via the canula as well, and she was dressed in a hospital gown. A large white dressing adorned her head where the wound was, but apart from that, she looked quite normal.

"Hello, you," Lyons said, as Fahy sat up awkwardly.

"Hi, boss. Thanks for coming in."

Lyons went to the bedside and gave her sergeant an affectionate hug.

"It's Maureen in here, Sally. How the hell are you feeling?"

"A bit groggy, but OK. It's not as bad as it looks. But I have a horrible headache. The doctor says I will have that for a few days. They've given me stuff for it, but it hasn't really worked."

Lyons sat down in the chair beside the bed and reached out to take Fahy's hand.

"God, you poor thing. What the hell happened?"

"Well, I'm sure Pascal told you, he'd just popped back to his house to get his phone. Apparently, he'd left it at home. Anyway, he wasn't gone long when the door of my car was wrenched open, and this bloke dragged me out by my hair. I've no idea where he came from; he was just there all of a sudden. Anyway, as soon as he got me out of the car, he picked up a convenient rock, and whacked me across the back of the head. That's it. Lights out for Sally – and here I am."

"Jesus, that's awful. Pascal is mortified, of course. He blames himself for it all. Anyway, I think we have your rock-wielding friend in custody, at least I hope it's him."

"Wow – that was quick. What's the story?"

"Not sure yet. We're going to question him at ten in the morning. I think it's all tied up with this Durnan thing, but I haven't figured it out yet. Did they say how long you'll be in for?"

"They hinted they might let me out tomorrow evening, but it depends on what progress I make today."

"And me sitting here talking at you probably doesn't help. Listen, I'll go on, if you don't mind. I've been up all night too, and I need to get a couple of hours' rest before the interrogation starts. Text me when you know what's happening, and I'll come and get you. And you can stay at ours for a few days till you're fit again, if you like."

"Thanks, Maureen, that's very kind of you. And thanks again for coming in."

Chapter Twenty-Seven

The interrogation of the two suspects started at ten o'clock the following morning. As arranged, Eamon Flynn took Fintan, and Lyons went to talk to Shauna Durnan.

Lyons had brought a uniformed Guard into the interview room to record what was being said. Of course, they now had tape recorders, but the law still required them to write everything down longhand.

"Well, Shauna. Let's see if we can find out what's been going on here, shall we? Firstly, you told me previously that you didn't have a boyfriend, yet you were found at your aunt's house in bed with Fintan. What's the story there?" Lyons said.

"He's not really a boyfriend. He just helps us out and we kind of got close over the last month or two," the girl said defiantly.

"OK. So, what do you know about him, then?"

"He's a really nice guy. He's from the town. He helps me with the stables and mucking out the horses, and he can ride too. He often takes one of them out for a gallop."

"I suppose you know that we suspect him of carrying out a very serious assault on a Garda officer out in Connemara. He left the poor girl for dead in the ditch and ran away," Lyons said.

"He was scared, that's all. He didn't mean to hurt her."

"Scared. Scared of what, Shauna?"

The girl looked down at her feet. She was thinking about how much she should tell Lyons.

Lyons read the signs well. She had seen this before, and she reckoned Shauna might just be about to blurt out the whole story, so she remained silent, waiting for Shauna to gather the courage to speak again.

"You don't understand, Inspector. My dad wasn't the nice, kind, gentle man that everybody thought he was. He had a terrible temper, and if things didn't go well for him at the races, he took it out on Mum and me."

"When you say 'took it out' what exactly do you mean, Shauna?"

"He hit us. Especially Mum. He often punched her in the gut and pulled her hair. It was terrible. He'd come home and set about a bottle of whiskey. Then, when he had half of it drunk, he would flare up and start throwing his fists around," Shauna said, fighting to hold back tears.

"And did he hit you too?"

Shauna was looking down at the table now, but she nodded visibly without saying anything.

"I see. How often did this sort of thing go on, Shauna?"

Shauna looked up again.

"Every couple of weeks. And that's not all either."

Another long silence followed. Eventually, Lyons prompted her to continue.

"He was at me too."

"What do you mean, Shauna. How was he 'at you'?"

"He used to come to my room late at night and get into bed with me. I hated it. He stank of whiskey. But he was strong. There was no way I could resist him when he was in that humour."

"Are you saying he raped you, Shauna?"

The girl looked down at the table again and nodded.

"What age were you when this started, Shauna?"

"Fourteen. We'd had a great day at Limerick Races and he made pots of money. We stopped on the way home and he started drinking then. When we got home he continued with the whiskey, and then later that night he came into my room and it happened. I was terrified."

"Does your mother know about this?"

"Yes, she does. But she couldn't do anything. She was very frightened of him too. He beat her pretty badly when the humour was on him."

"I see. And there was no one you could tell, or get help from?"

"No. Of course not. No one would believe us anyway. He was so charming when he was out and about. But it was a different story indoors."

"I see. I'm sorry you had to put up with that, Shauna. Tell me. How did Fintan get involved?"

"He came into the stables one time when dad was doing it to me. He saw what was happening. I was crying and trying to get him to stop – but there was no stopping him when he was like that. Dad lost his cool altogether. He fired Fintan on the spot and told him if he said anything to anyone, he would be sorry. But I stayed in touch with Fintan by phone, and I saw him occasionally in the town."

"Did Fintan say anything about doing anything to your father?"

"Not in any specific terms. But he said he would deal with him. I thought it was just all talk, but maybe he took it further."

"Do you think Fintan had anything to do with your father's death?"

Again, Shauna looked down at her feet and nodded.

"I see. Did he tell you what happened?"

More nodding.

"He said that what Dad was doing really started to eat into him after he was fired. He couldn't bear the thought of me being molested like that, and he knew Dad hit my mum as well. So he made a plan to attack him one evening after the racing had finished in Galway. I don't think he intended to kill him. He just wanted him to stop what he was doing."

"Did you know what he was planning, Shauna?"

"No, I didn't. He only told me afterwards. That's when I agreed to help him get away. I knew all about the stash of money in the stables, so I was going to give it to him and he was going to go to England for a while. I was to join him there later."

"And what about that business out in Roundstone. What happened there?"

"He was hiding out in the old caravan park. His parents used to go there when he was small for holidays, so he knew where it was. Then, when he saw the car parked up behind the wall, he got frightened. He thought you were on to him, so he had to deal with it. He didn't mean to hurt the policewoman. Is she OK?"

"No, not really, Shauna. She's in hospital. But she'll live."

"God, I'm sorry. Really, I didn't mean for any of this to happen, though I'm not sorry Dad is gone. He was a brute. What will happen to us?"

"That's not for us to decide, Shauna. We just gather the evidence to put before the court at a later stage. I think we should take a break now. We'll get you some refreshment, and I'll be back in about half an hour. Are you sure you don't want a solicitor?"

Shauna shook her head.

When Lyons got back to the open plan, Eamon Flynn was there at his desk having a cup of coffee from a cardboard cup.

"How goes it, boss?" he said to Lyons.

"Pretty good, so far. She's told me a lot. Puts your lad rightly in the frame. What are you getting from Fintan?"

"Nothing. Not a dicky-bird. Someone has told him to stay quiet, so he hasn't said a word."

"OK. Well, leave him for now. When I've finished with Shauna, we'll both have a go at him. When he hears what she has told me, it may loosen his tongue. I'm going to take Valerie White back in with me. I think Shauna may know about the money angle Durnan was involved with."

Half an hour later, Lyons went back in for round two with Shauna Durnan, accompanied by Valerie White. Lyons introduced the inspector, and, when they were all seated, she said to Shauna, "Now, Shauna, I'd like you to tell us about the money."

"What do you want to know?"

"Well, there was clearly quite a large stash of ready money hidden in the stables. How did that get there?"

"That was Dad's secret fund. He was cooking his books at the races with some other fellas he got in with, and that was what he had skimmed off."

"How did that work?" White asked.

Shauna went on to explain the scam that they had been running to launder money, and how her father had accumulated a lot of cash as a result.

"A guy would approach him with a sort of coded message during the meeting. It usually involved a bet on the last race of one or two grand. Dad waited till the race was over and then wrote it up as a win. Simple really. But he wasn't happy about it," Shauna said.

"Why not?"

"They were getting greedy. He had to pay them after every meeting recently. On the way home, we'd stop off at that dreadful garage on the Tuam Road and give Brendan Moran a couple of grand. Dad said Moran was making more out of him than he was making himself sometimes. But they had a hold on Dad by then. They told him if he didn't pay up, they would shop him to Revenue, and then he'd lose the house and everything, and he'd go to jail. He was furious."

"Did he keep any records of these payments, Shauna?" White said.

"No, course not. That would have been daft!"

"How much was in the hidey-hole?"

"I don't know. I stuffed as much as I could into the bag when we were leaving Nutfield, but I didn't count it. I suppose there must have been twenty thousand anyway."

"And you were going to give that all to Fintan?" White asked.

"Yes, of course. We were going to meet up in England, and the money was to get us settled in a place till we could get work."

Valerie White looked across at Lyons knowingly before they resumed questioning.

The interview went on for another half-hour with the Gardaí getting a bit more information from Shauna about the whole set up. They established that Jessica Durnan was not really involved with Fintan and his murderous plan. Shauna said that she was a weak woman who was unable to stand up to her controlling husband, and as a result had let serious matters go unreported over several years.

After lunch, Lyons and Flynn had another go at Fintan Casey. Armed with a very full statement from Shauna Durnan, they questioned him about how he had come to whack the bookie over the head at the racetrack, killing him.

"What exactly was your intention when you drove out to the racecourse that evening, Fintan?" Lyons asked.

With the evidence Shauna had provided, there was little point in him staying quiet any longer, and the two detectives felt that Fintan was relieved to be able to get the story off his chest.

"I never meant to kill him. I was just so angry at what he was doing to Shauna and her mother, and I didn't want him to get away with it any longer," Fintan said.

"So, how was bashing him over the head with a brick going to help?" Flynn asked.

"I dunno. He was just such a bastard. He needed taking down a peg or two."

"So, just to be completely clear, you admit to attacking John Durnan at Galway Racecourse and hitting him over the head with a brick?" Flynn said.

"Yes, I suppose so. But I didn't mean to kill him, right? I was going to put him in the back of the van and take him to a remote spot out near Roundstone, strip him bare, and dump him in the bog to teach him a lesson. But I heard someone coming after he fell to the floor, so I scarpered."

"And do you also admit to assaulting a police officer out at Dog's Bay causing her actual bodily harm?" Lyons said.

"I guess so. I was scared. I thought they were going to arrest me, so when the big lanky fucker left her on her own, I took my chance, didn't I?"

"What was your intention on that occasion, Fintan?" Flynn asked.

"I just wanted to get away, so I had to put her out of action for a while, that's all."

The interview continued with Lyons asking Fintan Casey how he came to buy a van from Brendan Moran.

"Shauna gave me some money, 'cos I knew I needed a big van to get Durnan out to the bog. I heard Moran did some good deals, so I went there and bought the Volks."

"You weren't aware of any connection between Durnan and Moran, then?" Lyons said.

"No, 'course not. I just wanted a cheap van for a few days. Then I swapped it with that eejit Deasy for the white Ford. He hasn't a clue."

"Did you know the VW was stolen?" Flynn asked.

"No. But I knew it was cheap."

Chapter Twenty-Eight

When the interviews had been completed, the detectives all met up in the office to discuss how they would process the suspects.

Lyons stood at the front of the room to address the team.

"So, what exactly have we got on this lot, then?"

Flynn was the first to speak.

"Well, we've got Casey banged to rights for manslaughter and assaulting a police officer, at least. And maybe we could tack on receiving stolen goods as well, if we need to."

"What about the girl?" White said.

"That's a bit trickier. We might be able to get her on conspiracy, but it's not going to be easy to prove," Lyons said.

"What about aiding and abetting?" White said.

"Did she, though? I'm not convinced that she knew what Casey's intentions actually were, and all she really did was to go with him well after the event with her father's ill-gotten gains. She could always claim duress there, too."

"Are you saying we have to let her go?" Flynn said.

"She's been through an awful lot at the hands of her father, Eamon. And I don't think the DPP would relish putting her up in court, if all that was going to come out during the trial. I'll have a word with Superintendent Hays, but I'd say we'll have to release her without charge."

"What about the mother?" Flynn said.

"Poor woman. She's in for a rough time of it. I doubt the insurance company will be in any hurry to pay out on Durnan's life policy. And Valerie here may well be taking a good deal of her available wealth, on the basis that it's the proceeds of crime. So she'll be skint. And she'll have to face the reality of what her husband was doing to her daughter for years. But I don't think there are any charges we can bring against her, do you?" Lyons said.

"Hmm… probably not. So that just leaves us with Casey. The fall guy, you could say."

"Do you think the women manipulated him for just this outcome, Eamon?" Lyons said.

"Women! Manipulative! I couldn't possibly comment, boss," he said with a wry smile.

* * *

"Mick, it's me. Have you got a minute or two for a chat about this Durnan thing? It's doing my head in," Lyons said.

"Yeah, sure. Pop up."

Lyons ascended the stairs to the third floor where Mick Hays had his spacious office.

"Hi, come in. Coffee?" he said.

"No thanks, I'm awash with the stuff. I won't sleep for a month."

"What's on your mind?"

Lyons gave Hays a brief account of the interviews that had taken place, and her intentions about who should be charged with what.

"Sounds about right to me, hun. I don't think there's much mileage in charging the girl, from what you say. It's not acceptable to be prosecuting abuse victims, and I doubt the DPP would go for it anyway, though I think she may have had more involvement than she's letting on. Is there no forensics to tie her in?" Hays said.

"None. She's either very, very clever, or genuinely not much involved."

"Either way, it amounts to the same thing. What's White getting out of it all?"

"She's happy to have closed down Brendan Moran, and she'll take the cash the kids tried to make off with. It will go to help some underprivileged youth club somewhere. She says you never really get the big guys in her game. You just nibble away at the edges till they get fed up and move on."

"So cynical for one so young!" Hays said.

"She's a realist," Lyons said. "Has she been speaking to you about this SOCU thing?"

"Just briefly. She has to make some observations when she gets back to town. I think they want to move on it quite quickly now. I've heard they want it up and running in January. Have you thought any more about it?" Hays said.

"You mean in between having one of my officers nearly killed and chasing around all over the bloody country after a pair of amateur murderers? Oh, sure, I've thought of little else!"

"Easy, girl. I just asked!"

"Yes, I know, sorry. I'm a bit wound up. Let's get this mess out of the way, and then we'll have a proper conversation about it. I'd welcome your input too."

"OK. Let's do that. Maybe we could get away for a weekend or something."

"Now you're talking. But we're not going to the bloody races – OK?"

* * *

Hays was as good as his word. They left Galway on Friday, late afternoon, and drove south to Killarney. He had booked them into the magnificent Great Southern Hotel, where every possible luxury was available to them.

Casey had been brought to court and remanded in custody until the Gardaí prepared their book of evidence. Lyons had assured Chief Superintendent Finbarr Plunkett that they had enough to get a conviction for manslaughter when it eventually came to court. It had been decided, after some consultation, not to charge Shauna Durnan with anything, and her mother was to be treated in the same manner.

The drive to Killarney was very enjoyable. They took the new M18 motorway to Limerick, bypassing Ennis and skirting Shannon Airport. As they drove past it, a Singapore Airlines Boeing 747 flew in low over them, temporarily drowning out their conversation.

Once they were past Limerick, they hit the beautiful little town of Adare. Hays never went through this town, but he thought of the murder of a serving Garda who had been cruelly shot in the village some years ago.

They drove on through Abbeyfeale and Castleisland, where the road divided around both sides of Sweeney's Emporium – the right-hand road leading into Tralee while the left-hand turn took them on towards Killarney. It was almost nine o'clock when they pulled up in front of the hotel, but once they had unloaded their bags and checked in, they were still in time for a delicious meal, which by that time they were both ready to devour.

On Saturday morning they rose at half past nine and enjoyed a magnificent breakfast, before heading out on foot to visit Muckross House. As they strolled along the road, Hays asked Lyons about her decision concerning the SOCU.

"Listen, Mick, truth now; do you think I'd be able to do it?" Lyons said.

"I can't think of anyone that would do better, and that's the truth, Maureen."

"Really? God, I don't know, Mick. But I suppose if Valerie White can cut it, I should be able to handle it."

"I agree. And there's something else you should know," Hays said.

"What's that?"

"Plunkett has put in a very strong recommendation for you. I know he thinks you're a bit of a maverick sometimes, but he's very impressed with your results. And why not, after all."

"Really! That surprises me. Maybe he just wants to get rid of me."

"Don't be so self-deprecating. You've done the force a lot of good out West, and he reckons it would be a feather in his cap to have you selected for SOCU."

"Hmm. OK. Maybe I'll give it a go, then. How does it all work?"

"Well, there's an interview process, but that will be almost a formality. You might have to go through some tests around firearms and driving, that sort of thing. But to be honest, they'll have made up their minds long before all that palaver."

"Cool. Now, here's the hard question. What would you think of it all – as my partner, not as my senior officer. Would you be happy to have me caught up in all that nastiness?"

"Naturally, I'd be concerned – especially when some of the trickier operations were underway. But if it's right for you – and I think it probably is – I wouldn't stand in your way. But I wouldn't be able to provide much top cover for you – not that I've had to do much of that anyway."

Lyons took his hand and squeezed it firmly.

"You're a good man, Mick Hays. Sounds like a done deal, then, doesn't it?"

Epilogue

Detective Sergeant Sally Fahy recovered from her ordeal at the hands of Fintan Casey out at Dog's Bay. She took Lyons up on her invitation, and when she was discharged from hospital, she went to stay with Hays and Lyons for a few days at their house in Salthill. After some long, bracing walks by the sea, and as much good food as Hays could get her to eat, Fahy was as good as new within a week, and moved back to her own place in the city. She was very grateful to her bosses for their consideration, and said as much, even buying them a generous gift of a case of fine wine before she departed.

Fintan Casey was brought to court a few months later on charges of manslaughter and assaulting a police officer. His barrister argued that he was a young and naïve individual who had been manipulated by two devious women with their own agenda, and he hinted that sexual favours had been exchanged for the elimination of a domineering and brutal husband and father. The judge asked why these two women were not also before the court, which brought a swift end to that particular line of defence. Nevertheless, Casey's boyish appearance struck a chord with the jury, and in the end, he was convicted and sentenced to eight years in prison, with the last two years suspended.

After a good deal of discussion and consultation with the DPP, it was decided not to bring charges against the Durnans. Inspector White seized the cash that had been recovered from Fintan Casey and Shauna Durnan's rather pathetic attempt to avoid capture. It was deemed to be the proceeds of crime, and was handed over to the Criminal Assets Bureau. White was also quite content that they had closed down the rogue car dealer, Moran, and she left the city pleased that she had enough to keep her superiors happy.

The life insurance company that held John Durnan's policy were reluctant to pay out, hiding behind the notion that, in law, no one can profit from their own crime. But Jessica Durnan hired a good solicitor on a 'no foal – no fee' basis, and it was pointed out that Mrs Durnan hadn't actually been charged with a crime, so that excuse was invalid. Eventually, the company settled for half the value of the policy. The solicitor took ten percent for his trouble, so Jessica Durnan was left with a little over a hundred thousand to restart her life as a widow.

Shauna took over her father's business. She knew it inside out in any case, and she was well known amongst the racing crowd. She kept Ronan, the clerk, on as well, but she ran the book completely straight, and didn't get involved in anything untoward. After a year or two plying her trade, she learned how to take on a horse, just as her father had, and she increased her earnings substantially by that means. They kept the house at Nutfield Cross, and Shauna purchased more horses as time went by.

* * *

In early September, when the fuss over Durnan's killing had died down, Chief Superintendent Finbarr Plunkett invited Mick Hays and Maureen Lyons up to his office. It was a cool autumn day, but sunny and bright, as it often is as soon as the children have gone back to school.

"Come in, Mick; Maureen. Take a seat. I have the coffee on the way. How are you both?"

"Grand, thanks, sir," Lyons replied for both of them.

"Well, now, I have some good news at last," Plunkett said. "We've cleared the last hurdle for the SOCU unit," he said, waving a sheet of official-looking paper at them.

"What's that, sir? Is it the funding?" Hays asked.

"It is, of course, Mick. Don't you know it's always the last thing to get sorted, but we're good to go now."

"That's great, sir. Well done," Lyons said.

"Well, I won't say it wasn't a bit tricky in parts. But you did a fine job with that Inspector White, Maureen. She was well on our side by the time she got back to Dublin. So, now, have you decided what you want to do yourself?"

"Yes, sir, I have. I'd like to be put forward for the SOCU, if that's still OK?"

"Good girl, Maureen. Of course it is. I'm looking to get it started in January. There'll be a month or so of training for you up in Dublin in November, and then we can get going, organising the rest of the team and getting set up with all that new-fangled equipment you'll be learning about."

"Have you any idea who else is going to be involved, sir?" Lyons asked.

"That's up to you, girl. You get to choose, but if you need any advice, I'd ask you to bear a couple of things in mind. We don't want to leave the detective unit stripped bare, and we'll need to include members from other areas in the West, such as Sligo and maybe Limerick. I'm hoping to bring it up to ten officers all told, but in the early stages, you may have to share with some of the detective units till we can get it fully staffed."

"Oh, I see, sir. And have you thought about where we will be located?"

"Yes, I have that covered. We'll use the overflow unit the OPW provided for us last year when this place was being refurbished. It's close by, but separate too, if you see what I mean."

"Oh, yes. That should be fine."

"Well, if that's all then, I'll let you get on. Good luck with it all, and Mick, keep me posted on how things are going, won't you?" Plunkett said.

"Of course, sir. Thanks."

When they had left Plunkett's office, they went to Hays' room just down the corridor.

"Congratulations! Well done you. You deserve it," Hays said taking Lyons in his arms and kissing her gently.

"God, I don't know, Mick. Do you really think I'm up to it?"

"Of course you are, Maureen. And now you get to call the shots – literally. SOCU get top priority with almost everything, and there are lots of other units that you can draw on if things get tough. I have every confidence in you."

"That sounds like something the Taoiseach would say just before he fires a TD!"

"Sorry, yes it does, doesn't it? But I mean it. You're well able for it. And I'll still be around to offer support, don't forget. But there's another thing going on here, too. You'll be the first female officer to be put in charge of such a prestigious group in the Gardaí. So, there's a big political dimension to it as well. Will you be able to handle that OK?"

"No, I bloody won't. You know how much I hate all that nonsense. They can all just fuck off with their political shite!"

"That's my girl! I love it! Now, Inspector, I'm taking you to a very long and very boozy lunch to celebrate."

List of characters

Senior Inspector Maureen Lyons – a feisty member of An Garda Síochána who may be headed for a well-deserved promotion.

Superintendent Mick Hays – Lyons' partner in life who enjoys sailing on Galway Bay in his spare time.

Chief Superintendent Finbarr Plunkett – a wily senior Garda who can navigate his way around the Garda management with apparent ease.

Inspector Eamon Flynn – an astute Garda who is tenacious and determined in his efforts to catch criminals.

Sergeant Sally Fahy – a pretty Garda who is dedicated to her work in the force and is keen to get on.

Garda John O'Connor – a technical wizard who loves exploring mobile phones and PCs to discover what the owners would rather he didn't.

Sinéad Loughran – a skilled forensic scientist who doesn't let her grim work spoil her good humour.

Sergeant Séan Mulholland – some think Séan is a bit beyond his sell-by date, but there's plenty of life left in him yet.

Garda Pascal Brosnan – a hard-working Garda who runs the station on the edge of Roundstone.

Garda Mary Fallon – Brosnan's new assistant who shows a lot of promise.

Garda Jim Dolan – Séan Mulholland's right-hand man.

Dr Julian Dodd – a senior pathologist with a quirky style.

John Durnan – a bookmaker who likes to make a little extra on the side.

Ronan – John Durnan's loyal clerk.

Jessica Durnan – John's long-suffering wife.

Shauna Durnan – John and Jessica's daughter, who loves horses and helps her father's business.

Fintan Casey – Shauna's boyfriend.

Ted Maguire – a very helpful bank manager.

Dónal Keogh – an unlucky punter.

Brendan Moran – a car dealer who deals in more than cars.

Tadgh Deasy – runs a small garage near Roundstone.

Inspector Valerie White – from the Serious and Organised Crime Unit.

Inspector Frank Hamill – finds himself a bit out of his depth in the west.

Joe Mason – the Garda dog handler.

Brutus – Joe's magnificent and intelligent German Shepherd dog.

Ray Cummins – the manager at the Galway Races.

Derry Devlin; Ultan Whelan; Liam Joyce; Superintendent Anselm Brennan; Sergeant Wallace – other members of An Garda Síochána.

If you enjoyed this book, please let others know by leaving a quick review on Amazon. Also, if you spot anything untoward in the paperback, get in touch. We strive for the best quality and appreciate reader feedback.

editor@thebookfolks.com

www.thebookfolks.com

BOOKS BY DAVID PEARSON

In this series:

Murder on the Old Bog Road (Book 1)
Murder at the Old Cottage (Book 2)
Murder on the West Coast (Book 3)
Murder at the Pony Show (Book 4)
Murder on Pay Day (Book 5)
Murder in the Air (Book 6)
Murder at the Holiday Home (Book 7)
Murder on the Peninsula (Book 8)
Murder at the Races (Book 9)

All of these books are free with Kindle Unlimited and available in paperback.

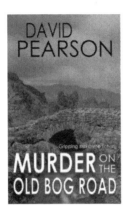

A woman is found in a ditch, murdered. As the list of suspects grows, an Irish town's dirty secrets are exposed. Detective Inspector Mick Hays and DS Maureen Lyons are called in to investigate. But getting the locals to even speak to the police will take some doing. Will they find the killer in their midst?

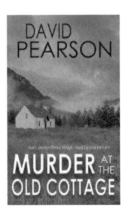

When a nurse finds a reclusive old man dead in his armchair in his cottage, the local Garda surmise he was the victim of a burglary gone wrong. However, having suffered a violent death and there being no apparent robbery, Irish detectives are not so sure. It will take all their wits and training to track down the killer.

When the Irish police arrive at a road accident, they find evidence of a kidnapping and a murder. Detective Maureen Lyons is in charge of the case but, struggling with self-doubt, when a suspect slips through her fingers she must act fast to save her reputation and crack the case.

A man is found dead during the annual Connemara Pony Show. Panic spreads through the event when it is discovered he was murdered. Detective Maureen Lyons leads the investigation but the powers that be threaten to stonewall the inquiry.

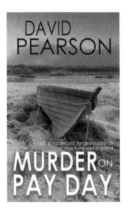

Following a tip-off, Irish police lie in wait for a robbery. But the criminals cleverly evade their grasp. Meanwhile, a body is found beneath a cliff. DCI Mick Hays' chances of promotion will be blown unless he sorts out the mess.

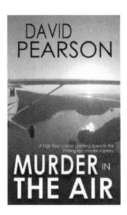

After a wealthy businessman's plane crashes into bogland it is discovered the engine was tampered with. But who out of the three occupants was the intended target? DI Maureen Lyons leads the investigation, which points to shady dealings and an even darker crime.

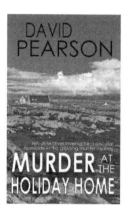

A local businessman is questioned when a young woman is found dead in his property. His caginess makes him a prime suspect in what is now a murder inquiry. But with no clear motive and no evidence, detectives will have a hard task proving their case. They'll have to follow the money, even if it leads them into danger.

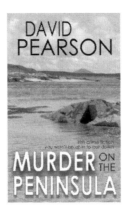

When a body is found on a remote Irish beach, detectives suspect foul play. Their investigation leads them to believe the death is connected to corruption in local government.

But rather than have to hunt down the killer, he approaches them. With one idea in mind: revenge.

Printed in Great Britain
by Amazon

39095803R00125